Beyond the Mirage

Praise for BEYOND THE MIRAGE

"A beautifully written exploration of faith that elevates the contemporary Christian genre and finally takes us somewhere new."

-BRAD PAUQUETTE

FOUNDER AND DIRECTOR OF **THE COMPANY**

AND BESTSELLING AUTHOR OF **THE NOVEL MATRIX**

"A novel that will have you laughing and crying in the same breath."

-NOAH J. MATTHEWS

AUTHOR OF **OUTLAW BLOOD**

"An amazing debut novel from Vella Karman. This story perfectly captures struggles with faith, trust, and the intimidating yet powerful act of stepping into the calling God has for you. Keep an eye out for more from her in the future, because Vella's just getting started!"

-ALLI PRINCE

BESTSELLING AUTHOR OF **COPPER LIES**

AND **CALL IT CONSEQUENCES**

BEYOND THE MIRAGE

Vella Karman

The Pearl Factory, LLC
dba The Pearl
303 N. 7th St.
Cambridge, OH 43725
www.PearlMag.co

Developmental Editor
BRAD PAUQUETTE

Copy Editor
NOAH MATTHEWS

Book Designer
ALLI PRINCE

Cover Artist
LEVI MATTHEWS

Copyright © 2026 by Vella Karman LLC. All rights reserved. This book, or parts thereof, may not be reproduced in any form without permission.

LCCN: 2026937023

Print ISBN: 978-1-960230-25-6
E-book ISBN: 978-1-960230-27-0

To my sister—Adi, you mean the world to me.

I TURNED ON MY BLINKER like I was about to jump off the diving board for the first time. Sweat dripped down my neck and plastered red curls to my skin. "Do you see anyone?" I asked my friend in the passenger seat.

Hazel sat up straight and craned her neck. "It's clear."

I took a deep breath and steered the RV into the right lane of a four-lane highway. Only scattered cars remained in sight across the stretch of Arizona desert shimmering through the windshield. The RV resisted my steering like a cat on a leash. I'd told Grandpa Mack he was better at driving it than me.

I wished he was behind the wheel. Or literally anyone else.

As if insulting my wish, the *buzz, buzz, buzz* of a snore wound its way into my ears from the living room area behind us. I pulled my sweat-soaked olive-green tank top away from my skin so air could circulate underneath. "Is everyone asleep back there?"

Hazel twisted in her seat. "Pretty much."

She yawned.

On the road ahead, a puddle of filthy oil shifted into focus. I jerked my head to check that the left lane was still clear before I veered onto it to avoid the slick black goop.

Heat shimmered down from the sun, highlighting the sand and scraggly bushes laid flat around us on every side. The Clipper Mountains barring our way into California looked like shadows in the distance—blue shimmering mirages in the heat.

I dropped my tank top and it snapped against my skin again. I sighed. "July weddings."

"Brave," Hazel said.

I glanced at her silhouette in the farthest corner of my vision. "What do you mean?"

Her chin jutted out from between her pixie-cut curls. "Moving to California."

We'd passed the oil puddle, where some poor unfortunate car had probably broken down in the desert. I wondered what had happened to those people as I returned to the right lane. "It's not like she has a choice. His mom's an invalid."

The RV rattled, filling the silence that followed my statement.

"What about *his* in-laws? Are *they* invalids?" a voice from the backseat called.

I jumped at the unfamiliar voice and hit the rumble strips. Out of the corner of my eye I saw Xavier stagger like a drunk as he made his way to the front.

He had been sitting next to his girlfriend on the couch built into the passenger side wall. Grandpa Mack sat in the diner-style booth across the way from the couch and directly behind the driver's seat.

I had met Xavier just a few hours before, but the only flicker of interest he'd shown towards anything other than his girlfriend was the grudging respect in his gaze when he'd heard Grandpa Mack was a quodesher.

Xavier's two bare hands gripped the headrests of the front seats.

Hazel glanced at the callused fingers next to her head. She unbuckled and stood, raising her phone in my direction.

After she disappeared into the living space behind us, Xavier plopped into the passenger seat. He crossed his lanky legs as he slouched. He didn't bother buckling. "So they're already there?"

"Who?"

"Your parents." He leaned back in the passenger seat and seemed to wait for me to start squirming.

I clenched my teeth.

He pulled a pen from his pocket and started clicking it with agonizing slowness. Cliiiiick-click. Cliiiiick-CLICK.

His hair flopped over his eyes as he smirked.

Close behind me, I spotted a vehicle gaining ground. The little rearview camera on the RV was fuzzy, but workable. There was no way I could miss the zippy red car on my tail.

Please pass me—I'm in the right lane, I pleaded with the driver silently.

"Are your parents coming?"

I risked a glance at Xavier. "Why do you want to know? You just met me."

He spun the pen in his hand, again with agonizing slowness. "It's weird. A wedding with no mention of one whole set of in-laws? It should be against the law."

I checked the little screen on the dashboard. Below the image of the red car gaining ground from the rearview camera, buttons covered the space behind the steering wheel and the middle console.

The roar of the red car revving its engine behind us filled my ears.

My heart started beat-beat-beating in my chest.

"You don't seem like a curious person," I said, gripping the steering wheel with white knuckles. I pressed the gas pedal deeper into its grooves and the engine responded from the dark bowels of the machine under my power. We sped up.

"Trust me, he is. I repeatedly remind him that curiosity killed the cat and he still never listens to my wise advice." The shrill voice reached over the seats, more familiar than Xavier's to my ears. Ava, my sister's best high school friend and Xavier's girlfriend, had an unreadable tone. Annoyed or amused? I couldn't tell.

As she spoke, Xavier started reaching towards the quodesh dial.

It hovered a few inches over the dashboard, a small compass-sized dial with edges defined by bright, bright light. Trying to look at them directly was like trying to look at the sun.

The part you twisted was the size of a washing machine dial, made of a crystal-like substance with a white arrow inside. On the slices of the dial, eight different state abbreviations showed in the same white lettering, raised on beautiful backgrounds like they weren't quite attached.

The arrow pointed to AZ.

Xavier sliced his hand through the air underneath the quodesh dial, then the air above it. His jaw lengthened as he studied it. "Huh, it really floats."

I checked the rear-view camera. The zippy red car still clung to my tail. How rude.

I'm going seventy-five, what do you want from me?

I couldn't reach eighty in this old RV without the risk of breaking down—couldn't they see that? I wanted to hit the brakes and force them to go around, but they were tailgating me by now. We might be rear-ended if I slowed. So I held the pedal at a steady seventy-five.

Please do something, please do something, I pleaded in my head. If only the driver could hear me.

I gripped the wheel harder and stared at the mountains in the distance. They looked like cut-outs in a multi-media craft project.

That was a good idea...I should use it when I'm a teacher someday. I smiled at the thought...buckets of glue and construction paper turned into a natural geography lesson.

Xavier continued to pass his hand back and forth underneath the floating quodesh dial. His fingers were long and strong, like his face. His dark hair flopped in a gentle wave all the way to his chin in a kind of surfer boy hairstyle.

I couldn't help but notice it looked softer than mine.

He made eye contact and grinned as if to say, "I know, the girls can't resist."

I turned my head back to the road again and sucked in a sharp breath. I hated guys who had good looks but not good character.

He touched the crystal handle of the dial. "What happens if I turn it?"

"Nothing."

Xavier twisted the dial with a dramatic flick of his wrist. He waited a second and when nothing happened, he tapped the back of my arm with his pen.

I moved my hands higher on the steering wheel and glared.

"Why only eight options? Doesn't it go to every state?" he asked.

I set my teeth.

Grandpa Mack's wise, calm voice carried from the booth a few feet behind us. "Turn 'em farther round, Xavier. Yer a few clicks from all fifty states. Washington DC is there iffen you turn far 'nough."

I hadn't noticed when the snoring stopped. Simply the sound of him speaking relaxed my shoulders and unset my teeth. At least until I glanced in the mirror and saw the red car still tailgating.

Xavier twisted the dial all the way around and leaped backwards, thudding into the faux leather of the seat. "What the—" He peered closer at the dial. "They changed! What the—did you see that, Ava?"

She must've nodded because I didn't hear a response.

I glanced at the dial. It was set for OH, a sparkling pink pie slice. "Grandpa Mack, don't we need to move it back to Arizona or we'll be somewhere else when we get off on the next exit?" I didn't dare glance in the mirror to see Grandpa Mack's face as I caught a whiff of fear in the tone of my voice.

"Yer right. She oughtta be set to Arizona fer now," Grandpa Mack said.

"Please flip it back this instant Xavier," Ava whined. "I have no desire to explore when I feel motion sick. We're traveling incredibly fast."

I squeezed the steering wheel until my knuckles strained white. I could slow the RV if only the zippy red car would pass us.

Xavier rolled his eyes and turned the dial clockwise like he had before.

"Not that way." I piped up. "Not unless you want to go through every single one."

That had been my pastime when I was in elementary school... turning the dial round and round and round and imagining all the places I'd go when I was old enough to drive someday.

My stomach turned.

Xavier continued to twist the dial in his direction, taking a full minute of twist-twist-twisting to reach the ravishing ruby section marked for AZ.

Hazel returned to the cab, her sunshiny presence welcome. She pointed to Xavier sitting on top of the seatbelt. “My seat?”

As they traded places, Xavier heading back to his girlfriend, I realized his hair was longer than Hazel’s. Only hers was straight unless she curled it.

She sat and I glanced at her profile. She had a nose like every seven-year-old puts in a drawing. Strong straight lines sized just perfectly for her face, curved eyebrows, and a smile that brightened the day of every person who walked into the Phoenix Chick-fil-A.

The RV rattled like a child’s toy. I took a deep breath and words poured out of me like churning water. “Hazel, there’s a car tailgating the RV and it won’t change lanes and pass us. What can I do?”

“Use the other lane,” she said as she buckled her seatbelt.

My mouth dropped open. “Thank you, Hazel!”

I turned on my blinker, pressed the gas pedal even harder, checked over my shoulder, and shifted lanes.

The red car stayed in my blind spot, unyielding in its desire to be in my space, like some fly attracted to my hair and circling me in lazy droning loops, pincers waving in the breeze.

“Hey!” Ava called from the main area of the RV. She sprawled on the couch with Xavier’s arm wrapped around her shoulders and pieces of curly girl hair sprouting from her head in black ringlets. “I need to use a restroom so you must stop if there’s any places anywhere soon.”

Xavier piped up. “Mr. Roche, can we—”

“My name’s not Roche, son.” Grandpa Mack’s voice rang like the final toll of a bell.

I willed myself not to swerve while I peered in the center mirror.

Ava’s apple pink cheeks stood out next to her boyfriend’s tanned skin. One ringlet, cut short into a bang, strayed onto her forehead.

Grandpa Mack looked cool as a cucumber as he placed a bookmark in his paperback. The tufts of his white and gray beard jutted over the collar of a faded yellow button-up shirt. His whiskered cheeks hid the upturned corners of his mouth, and his salt and pepper mane distinguished his forehead. “Call me Grandpa Mack. Iffen ya need titles.”

Xavier swiveled his head towards me.

I turned back to the road, surprised to see the hood of the red car even with me in the other lane. I checked the speedometer: 72. I’d slowed down without realizing it.

I let off the gas even more, falling to 69 so they would finally pass me.

“Grandpa Mack,” Xavier started, car salesman charm tinting his voice even through the genuine respect, “can we quodesh to New York so my girlfriend can go?”

I imagined Grandpa Mack shaking his head, pulling his wire framed reading glasses from his face and setting them on the miniature table in the middle of the booth.

He sat in the farther seat of the booth, his face towards the front of the vehicle. If I hadn’t been so diligently scanning the road for new cars that weren’t there, I could’ve seen his face in the mirror.

I imagined the wire framed glasses settled atop the chipped orange cover of his paperback biography of Bonhoeffer.

Grandpa Mack’s presence was such a comfort. Even though he’d messed up my plans, having him awake made it easier to handle everything.

The flashy red car finally edged past me and zoomed ahead into the mirage of water pooling in the distant road.

The tenor tones of Xavier’s voice continued. “I bought a ride in a quodeshing car once. It only took ten minutes to teleport from Arizona to Florida and back.”

"Son, that's not what quodeshing is fer."

I checked my speed, settling for a comfortable 65 mph on the dumpy bumpy road stretching from here to the mountains and through the facades of sparkling water in the middle distance.

I glanced in the rearview mirror.

Grandpa Mack was rolling up the cuffs of his shirt as he talked, his eyebrows pinching together over the bridge of his nose. "Quodeshing's a powerful thing. It's not fer play. With yer great power comes yer great responsibility."

Hazel elbowed me. "Glad he made you drive?" she whispered.

"What?" I checked the road again, swiping beads of sweat from my forehead with my forearm. The AC was broken in the old RV.

She lowered her voice even more. "Imagine you were back there. You'd be answering Xavier's questions." Each word in her last sentence was like a poke in the face.

I peered at the screen showing me the rearview camera feed.

A distant car approached, the sun's rays glinting off the hood or the windshield, impossible to tell which at this distance.

I scrunched up my face to show Hazel I was thinking. She was probably right, only I didn't want to admit it. I was supposed to be holed up in the bedroom of the RV, working on assignments before the due dates rolled around at midnight. And when I'd finished that, I was supposed to have Grandpa Mack to myself.

I tuned into the backseat conversation again.

Xavier's tone challenged Grandpa Mack with every question. "Is only your RV equipped? Can your other cars quodesh?"

"All of 'em," Grandpa Mack said.

"Huh. That must cost you hundreds."

I peeked in the rearview mirror, curious to hear his answer.

Grandpa's eyes twinkled as he buttoned his second shirt cuff, but he gave no response.

I turned back to Hazel, the salty sweat that had leaked into my mouth tasting like the lemon at the bottom of the glass. "I don't know what to do. I'm behind on assignments already."

Hazel fixed her eyes on me. "Tough. I'm glad I work."

"But you work all the time."

"My pleasure," she said wryly. "It's less stressful than staying at home."

The car I'd seen in the rearview camera approached the RV. I could see it clearly now—a silver Highlander with a black bumper that looked like nothing so much as a bulldozer's front loader.

I gripped the steering wheel as it approached. "Hazel, I can barely keep up with ONE college class." I swallowed, my fingers aching from their long tight curling around the steering wheel. "What if I bomb out when I get there?"

A picture of the last person I had asked that question to popped into my mind. Miss Eunice at the nursing home.

I'd seen her Monday when I'd gone with Grandpa to visit the residents, just before he'd volunteered to transport "all the young folk" from Phoenix, AZ—where we lived—to San Diego, CA, where the wedding would be held. Miss Eunice had worn a delicate pink cardigan and she'd remembered who I was.

Hazel looked at me in concern, or with empathy, I didn't know which. A little furrow on the bridge of her nose and a shift in her eyes clued me in—she felt sorry for me.

I sped up a little, realizing I'd dropped down to 60 mph and we'd never get to San Diego with enough time to shower before the rehearsal dinner at that rate. The silver car still gained on me. "I asked

Miss Eunice the same question, and you know what she said?"

Hazel shook her head.

"If you do flunk out of college, that might not be a bad thing," I repeated.

Miss Eunice had reached across the folding card table and patted my arm after she said it, the way a mom might, her palms wrinkly against my bare skin. "You can come back and spend more time with me and your family. Is it about the journey or the destination?" Her voice had creaked with age and wisdom as she said the last part, the part of journeys and destinations. From Miss Eunice, it didn't sound like a catchy phrase with no rhyme or reason to it, but I still had no clue how it was supposed to help.

Xavier's voice raised from the couches behind us, each word drawn out like a pen cliiiiicking and uncliiiiicking in slow motion. "Sir. Letting my girlfriend use the bathroom is a responsible cause, right?"

"This RV is old, son." Grandpa Mack patted the wall closest to him. "She's lasted fer ten years now. She might break down."

"She?" Hazel piped up, spine straightening and head whipping around to look at them. "She's named?"

"Naw," Grandpa Mack told her. "We oughtta though. Any of ya got an idea?"

Ava pulled her legs up onto the clear space of the sofa cushion next to her, black leggings and white high tops in two straight lines as she leaned back into Xavier. "I think she should be named Barbie, which is iconic."

Hazel twisted around in her seat, facing the rest of the group. "Barbie?"

Ava crossed her arms, wrinkling the oversized blue t-shirt draping from her shoulders like a blanket.

"Ya fine young folks can decide," Grandpa Mack said. He thoughtfully offered to trade spots with Hazel so's she could be part of 'er conversation.

The remains of a coyote littered the road ahead, the corpse lying on the yellow line and into my lane. I swerved around it, just remembering about the silver car in time to see I'd edged dangerously into their lane.

I jerked the steering wheel back, hitting the coyote's legs and jostling the RV as fresh blood pooled into the road. I fought to keep from closing my eyes with that sickening image seared into my brain and Grandpa Mack stumbled into the back of the driver's seat chair with an "oomph!"

"Oops." My stomach roiled, and it felt like blood was pooling in it the same way blood had pooled from the dead coyote's left claw.

"Yer alright, Lauren. Ya just keep on drivin'." Grandpa Mack held to the headrests as he moved to avoid falling if I swerved again.

I stared at the road ahead, scanning for roadkill or cars or anything else I should be aware of on that gray-blue road. All I saw were the yellow lines on either side of the freeway curving like long strings of spaghetti, a desert of cacti, and the blue, blue sky.

The silver car inched ahead of me. Although we were catty-corner now, I couldn't wait for that silver bumper to fade into the distance. I double checked my speed: 66 mph. *Okay...I should be good.*

"Comfy behind yer wheel now, sweetheart?" Grandpa Mack leaned into my vision, smiling his gentle smile. I wondered if he'd ever tamed a wild animal, because that smile should work just as well on a wounded animal as a startled eighteen-year-old.

I smiled my own sad smile at the dotted white line separating the two lanes of the road. "It's good practice for driving to CCU."

Grandpa settled back into his seat. "I'm proud yer confident. Now ya can go far."

I grabbed a glance of him from the corner of my eye, his sturdy frame relaxed in the big seat, his eyes alert on the road, his work-worn hands on his knees. "But what about you?"

"I'm where I'm supposed ta be." He released a gusty sigh. "Consequences don't matter, Lauren. Even when it turns wrong, ya know God put you there. We oughtta make peace with 'et."

He turned his head to the window then, admiring the scenery or hiding his sadness from me.

Green shrubs and cacti burst from the vibrant mustard-yellow sand like fingers grasping at the bright blue hue overhead.

Grandpa Mack's hair looked like a cloud in that sky, bundled together in a strong white pattern, interrupted by wisps reaching out to say hello to the ground and the highway and the heavens.

He sniffed and I felt like I saw his sadness reflected in the mountain range beyond him. The windshield framed them both, a painting hanging in a museum. Some masterpiece that little kids gawked at as their teacher explained the deep sad meaning.

I wondered why we tell kids about sadness in other people's lives, but we hide it from them in our own.

And I kept driving, like he told me to.

"Wherever we stop for gas can have the honor of the RV being named after it," Ava whined. "I desperately need to pee as soon as possible."

I'd forgotten about the RV-naming conversation. I guessed they'd been arguing for a long time at this point.

"Babe, it's okay." Xavier's lowered voice carried now that I'd started paying attention. I looked in the rearview mirror and saw him pop his head up like a groundhog playing peek-a-boo in the desert. "Hey

Mister—" He stopped and scrambled his words around real quick. "I mean, Grandpa Mack, doesn't this thing have a bathroom?"

Grandpa Mack turned from the window, level-headed as always. "No water in it. Sad to say. Yer gonna have ta wait."

Xavier leaned back against the seat and closed his eyes. "I'm napping then," he announced to no one in particular. Ava frowned at him.

I flung my attention back to the road.

Grandpa Mack nodded at me, as if to say, "You're doing alright, Lauren. You're doing alright."

"Grandpa Mack, what if we had a different car and it was safe. Would it be okay to quodesh to a bathroom then?" I glanced back at Ava biting her nails. "She really needs to go."

Grandpa Mack stroked his beard, considering. I loved it when he stroked his beard—it made him look like some jolly old English man planning a brilliant surprise.

"Like ya heard, great power an' responsibility. Yer quodesher responsibility's easy. 'Et's one question. Why did God give us this power?" Grandpa Mack chuckled and lowered his voice. "I know thet boy. He wants to brag. Say how many times he's been in a quodeshin' car. There's them people selling tickets. It's no amusement park." His unruly gray-and-white eyebrows lowered into a sharp crease. "Thet's wrong. Those people never asked the question. I don't understand why God allows thet."

He took a long inhale, the bracing after years of questioning. "The Lord's good. Iffen ya ask 'im, he'll answer thet question for ya."

"Seligman!" Ava cried. "Look everyone, finally I see an exit and the promise of sweet relief!"

SELIGMAN, AZ WAS CROWDED with signs and slogans like gemstones lining the sides of a mine. The locals had plastered "get your kicks on Route 66" across buildings, on official street signs, and probably on the postcards in the gas station we stopped at.

"Well now. I'll fill 'er up." Grandpa Mack patted my knee when I pulled to a stop and sighed in relief.

"I'm naming it Seligman in honor of this stop," Ava called as she hurried down the RV steps, self-importance propelling every footfall. Xavier disappeared with her.

Hazel paused in the doorway of the RV, the breeze whipping at her curls. She must've gotten up at four AM to use a curling iron on her hair before we left at five.

She stuck her hands in the pockets of her jean shorts as she dropped from the last step to the ground.

Only Grandpa Mack and I were still inside the RV.

The white door of the RV stood open to the breeze. Sunshine

poured in and puddled on the floor like a melted popsicle.

I stood between the two front seats and streeeeetched, surveying the inside of the RV.

To my right, a beige chair melded with a beige curtain. The curtain was tied tight, but when it hung closed, it covered the window next to the driver.

Beige fabric had been used to upholster the entire inside of the RV, and the rays of light spreading across it revealed splotches and stains.

The café-style table and benches—also just beyond the driver's seat—had the least stains and splotches of anything in the clunky old RV.

A tiny hallway joined the living room area with the bedroom tucked away at the back. The bathroom squeezed next to it, the door ajar as if elbowing the hallway.

A tiny kitchenette at the far left side of the living room area and a couch that seated two or three people rounded out the interior of the RV.

To my left, next to the couch, the open door swung in the breeze.

Grandpa Mack knocked against the dashboard with his knuckles, bringing my attention to where he sat in the passenger seat. "Go on. I'll take care o' good ol' Seligman."

"Seligman." I laughed. "Isn't that a boy's name?"

Grandpa Mack chuckled and hefted his weight into the driver's seat.

When my feet finally hit the gravel of the parking lot, I admired the slight glinting and sparkling in the emerald-green leaves of the single well-watered tree in the town.

As gas stations often do, this one had a section of grass for people to stretch their legs, dogs to relieve themselves, and this single tree to grow.

It was a mesquite tree...seven-foot-tall trunk with dark scraggly bark.

It would be so easy to climb, the wide strong branches bumping into each other like elbows and knees in a dogpile. But the only branches low enough to reach jutted at crazy angles too unstable to climb.

The seven-foot trunk was my problem. If I could just reach the middle branches, I could set up a tea party and invite fifteen guests to lounge on the branches.

My ringtone started blaring. "Suze" and a picture of my sister's glowing red hair showed on the screen.

Her voice rang in my ear like bells. "You are impossible, Lauren. Tell me why you haven't responded to my texts."

"I was driving."

"Why?"

"Grandpa Mack thought—"

She scoffed. "Oh seriously, you don't need to do everything he says."

"Well, I would've been too busy with *college* to respond to texts anyways." My heart beat-beat-beat in my chest.

I could hear the whistle of her inhaling through her teeth. "I need your support—it's the day before *my wedding*."

Silence flickered between us like a Chinese lantern spinning into the sky. "I'm sorry. What do you need?"

"The programs haven't arrived yet, and the wedding planner says we'll need to write them all by hand. *I* don't have time for calligraphy. But you will tonight after the rehearsal dinner."

"I...kinda need to finish some assignments."

"Seriously Lauren? Tell me they can wait a day or two."

Her words drop-kicked my pulse. I opened my mouth.

Suzannah's taut voice rang through the phone first. "Hold on, the caterer needs to ask me—yes sir?"

I strolled to the mesquite tree, standing under the shade of its branches as fabric scratched against the microphone and muffled the voices of conversation on the other side of my phone.

After a minute Ava and Xavier emerged from the gas station, hands clasped together. Ava flipped her hair and Xavier slouched as he walked, but they were laughing.

I found myself watching them.

I'd never dated before, and when my sister had dated Dennis they were both at Berkeley. Of course, Suzannah had told me a lot about it.

They'd met working together at an ice cream shop in the afternoons, they didn't have any classes together but still studied together, their first fight was about some campus rule, and their first kiss was in his dorm room.

But hearing about Suzannah's relationship over the phone was nothing like sitting in a car with Ava and Xavier.

Xavier was the newest boyfriend in a long string like beads on a bracelet, but I'd known Ava for years.

Ava and Suzannah had become friends soon after we moved to Phoenix.

In those days, I couldn't tell if Ava just tolerated me or even noticed my presence most of the time. She seemed pretty self-absorbed.

It was weird to actually *see* her with one of her boyfriends.

I heard a screech on the other end of the phone and my sister's voice burst through the muffled fabric. "It's a shame you can't fulfill what I paid for!"

I winced. *Poor caterer.*

Silence fell like a cloak on the other side of the phone. I shuffled my feet, kicking at dirt and grass around the base of the tree.

For some reason, this reminded me of a midnight phone call we had ages ago. She'd said: "It's a shame I can't marry this man tomorrow. Love has gotten its claws into me and won't let go!"

It wasn't the first time she'd said she was in love.

That night, she'd flopped onto the pillows of her couch with a thwomp. I had tuned her out as she started talking about kissing, but when he came to visit over Thanksgiving break a few weeks later, I'd paid close attention.

It seemed like he really cared for her. Like he could see past her dramatic front and admire the woman within. And that's when I'd decided Dennis was good enough for my sister.

I'd decided her last boyfriend was good enough for her too and they'd had an excruciating breakup, so I didn't fully trust my judgement yet, but I figured she had that covered.

On the other end of the phone, I stopped hearing voices. "Suze? Suzannah? Are you still there?"

Nothing.

I shrugged and hung up. My heart beat-beat-beat in my chest again.

Hazel emerged from the gas station, clutching a blue Gatorade bottle to her chest. She wore a ratty old Beatles t-shirt tucked into a pair of Bermuda jean shorts. Her pink flip flops slapped the pavement with each step.

She spotted me and came my way, clutching the Gatorade bottle as she twisted the lid.

The receipt clung to the side of the bottle, moisture turning the white paper clear where Hazel's hand pressed it against the plastic.

A black metal trash can decorated the sidewalk next to the gas station door. "There's a trash can over there if you want to throw that away." I nodded at the receipt.

Hazel folded it in half and forced it into the front pocket of her jean shorts. "No thanks." She gulped the Gatorade.

I approached the tree, brushing red-brown tangles away from my face. My olive-green tank top melded to my skin as the shade cooled my sweat. I gripped rough bark peeling away from the tree and tugged to test its strength. Yes, it held. It must've grown that way, the bark jutting out in grooves and solidified by time.

I stood a solid 5'6" without tennis shoes on, so if I jumped I could probably hit the bottom of the middle branches with my hand.

I planted one rainbow-colored Converse against the roots of the mesquite tree. Hugging the tree to gain more grip, I found footing for my left foot and hoisted myself higher. One whole inch higher.

Weeeee, I thought and laughed.

I turned my head, rubbing my cheek against the bark.

Hazel took another swig of the frosty blue Gatorade and gave me a thumbs up.

I hiked my left arm higher. My fingers found grip on some fungus-shaped fold of bark and I grabbed hold tightly.

A second foothold revealed itself in the dark shadows of the interlacing bark. Before I could dig my Converse into the gap, my other foot slipped.

I fell as Ava and Xavier joined us.

I stumbled backwards, a sharp pain sparking in my arm.

A raised red line was already forming on my skin where the bark had scratched my forearm.

Ava pointed into the interlacing network of branches which made the inside of the tree into a little alcove. "I want to sit up there in the shade! Xavier, give me a boost."

Xavier bumped me aside with his shoulder as he passed. I noticed he was only an inch taller than me, our shoulders almost level.

Xavier knelt in front of the tree on one knee.

Ava adjusted the dented silver watchband on her wrist. Her arms were bigger than mine, her muscles stronger, and one time she had helped Suzannah move the furniture around her room without Grandpa Mack's permission.

He hadn't cared the way a mom would have, but I guess they had felt rebellious.

She wasn't any taller than me, but she was sturdier.

Ava grabbed Xavier's right hand to steady herself and stepped onto the khaki shorts covering his left thigh. She wobbled to keep her balance on the flesh and bones beneath her.

After she got both feet on his leg, Xavier rose a few inches, his left arm braced against the tree to keep his balance. His right arm touched the backs of Ava's thighs, and his nose was terrifyingly close to her rear end as he peered upwards.

Ava grabbed at the tree with her right hand, trying to scrabble up the bark like a squirrel.

Xavier had taken my spot, so I circled the tree to find a new place to climb.

Almost everything on the other side of the trunk shone bare under the bright rays of sun flooding through the leaves. No major cracks, no high roots, nowhere to stick my fingers or the white-capped toes of my rainbow Converse.

I circled around to the others.

Xavier pushed Ava up none too gently as her left knee rested on his left shoulder—circus performers practicing a pyramid.

I tapped my foot against the grass, waiting for them to finish. The grass crunched under my foot, barely holding on to any green pigment in this heat.

Hazel sipped more Gatorade, the bottle half-empty now.

Grandpa Mack walked up to the tree, pocketing the keys to the RV.

Xavier turned his head towards us, Ava's knee still on his shoulder. “Wow, are you kidding me? You left the valuables alone? No one’s in the RV!”

Grandpa Mack patted the bulging shirt pocket just over his heart where he’d tucked the ring case. “Well now. I keep all my valuables right here.”

Xavier scowled. “There are cruise tickets in my wallet. Can’t someone watch the RV?” He made no move to hurry to the RV himself, but stared at Grandpa Mack, waiting for something.

“Ya oughtta bring yer wallet. Iffen yer worried, son.”

"SELIGMAN" CHUGGED ALONG at 60 miles an hour as we passed through the mountains. Heat waves continued to rise from the road as the morning crept along.

I glanced at the clock, my hands tightening on the steering wheel. *It's almost ten.* Five hours to go until San Diego. Maybe I'd have an hour or two to work before the reception...and then slaving away at programs for Suzannah until dawn.

Without a mom, sisters became many things to each other.

Back at the gas station, Grandpa Mack had given me a boost into the tree. I had settled on the opposite side of the trunk from Ava, swinging my legs and looking out over the parking lot.

A semi with a red cab had pulled up to the pumps, hitting the brakes with a hiss. I was glad the RV wasn't that big.

The semi driver had stepped out, a grizzly man who'd shoved the pump into his semitruck before lighting a cigarette.

I had raised my gaze past the parking lot and the white-capped plastic awning over the gas pumps, past the dark asphalt of the road and vrooming, zooming cars, past the signs and tops of buildings and to the open desert.

A wide expanse of dry heat had met my gaze, dust emanating from the sands, a stray tumbleweed spinning like a small dark merry-go-round against the horizon.

I had closed my eyes and sucked in a deep breath. *I'll miss the desert when I'm in Colorado.* But everything had felt right just at that moment...peaceful.

We'd been in the car two hours since then. Nothing much had happened except for Xavier clicking his pen over and over again and Hazel fielding another message from her boss who wanted her to come in.

In the living room area behind me, Grandpa Mack's phone started the tuneful jingle of his ringtone. "Well now. Hi Suzannah," he said.

The volume of his phone was turned up loud so's that it could reach his ears. Because of this, everyone in the RV heard every word Suzannah said.

"His mom might be having a stroke right now." Her tone pulsed with urgency. "What are we going to do? The wedding planner and caterers will kill me if we cancel now."

"Is she gettin' medical care?"

Suzannah scoffed. "The ambulance arrived a few minutes ago. Tell me this isn't happening the day before my wedding!"

"Calm down, sweetheart. We jest need to pray."

"I have to go," Suze said. She hung up without a goodbye.

The silence formed like an oil leak rising to the surface of the ocean.

"Do you think she'll be okay?" I asked.

Grandpa Mack sighed. "I'm prayin'. I jest can't tell."

A tight squeeze in my chest reminded me to look at the road.

Hazel was still on her phone, tethered to the charger in the bedroom at the back, so the passenger seat next to me was empty.

I needed to stretch my legs with a powerful urge that only came from driving for hours without fully straightening your leg on the gas pedal. I checked for cars around me. Seeing nothing but the dusty road descending into the desert I was leaving behind for a mountain pass, I looked in the mirror and caught sight of myself.

My eyes twinkled, like the lights from a far-flung town. I couldn't help looking like I knew some great secret about the world, the same way my sister couldn't help looking like a mourner unless she smiled for the picture.

I knew I was a dark-eyed beauty, with those brown eyes and red-brown hair, like bricks and wood and burnt umber got all mixed up on a painter's pallet.

In the rearview mirror, I caught sight of Grandpa Mack speaking into Xavier's ear. I called out a question: "How do I turn on cruise control, Grandpa Mack?"

Grandpa Mack leaned back in his seat, distancing himself from Xavier, and made eye contact with me in the mirror.

Xavier froze where he sat on the couch, his face unreadable but his eyes darting towards Grandpa Mack every few seconds.

"Press yer button on the wheel," Grandpa Mack called. He didn't have a booming, deep voice, so he actually had to raise his tuneful baritone for it to carry.

His voice started to creak with age, the way squeaky hinges had on the doors of the root cellar outside of our dirt-hut childhood home.

I shook that image from my head and scanned the steering wheel.

Little black buttons were wedged below the horn in the center of the wheel. A bunch of tiny white symbols decorated them, but they were as good as hieroglyphics to me. "Umm, which one?" I called back.

Grandpa Mack stood and made his way to the driver's area.

He thumped down into the passenger seat. I noticed he'd undone the top button of his shirt and the collar jutted out comfortably. He still wore his shirt tails tucked into his khakis, but with the sleeves rolled up and the top button undone.

He looked different than he usually looked after a workday.

He worked at an insurance office, the same one he'd worked at for the past thirty-five years, the same one that'd let him take time off to retrieve me and Suzannah when our parents died.

Grandpa Mack pointed at the steering wheel, the wrinkles on his knuckles standing out like bumps in the road. "Ya see the picture of a speedometer?"

Speedometer. I scanned the icons, glancing up at the road every few seconds. I put my finger on a button. "This one?"

"Try 'et, sweetheart. See what happens."

I made a face at him. Suddenly...pressing a button seemed like the hardest thing in the world. I punched it and pulled my finger away fast, like a toddler who'd touched a hot stove.

Nothing happened. I eased my foot off the gas pedal for a spit second before ramming it back into place. The RV jerked. "What now?" I turned to Grandpa Mack, who had braced his feet against the floor.

A little upturn at the corners of his mouth gave away the fact that he thought he was right, he thought he was placidly right, and I kind of hated that he probably was. "Take yer foot off the gas. That's after ya set the speed," he said.

I checked my rearview and blind spot, sheepishly feeling guilty that I hadn't done that before easing my foot from the gas pedal a few seconds before. I hadn't even tapped the brakes to signal that I might slow down. That could've caused an accident if I'd been anywhere but a deserted mountain highway.

After a minute of roaming the dashboard with my eyes, I found the place where the symbol on the button I had pressed showed up on the display screen.

A little "- - - mph" showed next to it.

I pressed the up and down arrow buttons on the steering wheel next to the cruise control button until the numbers on the screen hit 60 mph.

I glanced at Grandpa Mack and removed my foot completely from the gas pedal, my shoulders hunching as I waited for the impact.

I kept my grip tight on the steering wheel and my eyes on the white line to my left and the yellow line to my right. I heard a low growl as Seligman took control of his own speed.

We actually didn't jerk, although I felt the gears kick in under my feet and we sped up. It reminded me of riding my bike downhill on the steepest street in our neighborhood without training wheels.

Grandpa Mack grinned at me.

We started to round a turn and I snapped my eyes back to the road, carefully maneuvering in the middle of the lane. As we came out of the turn, I saw a black car parked on the side of the road ahead, partway in my lane.

I swerved, checking my blind spot as I went. Luckily no one was there and we hurtled past the car.

My gaze stayed on the car, wondering if anyone was inside. Now that we'd entered the curving roads of the highway mountain pass, shade pressed in on us for the first time in the pounding summer heat. The temperature had dropped and the sweat sliding from my armpits into the folds of my tank top began to ebb its flow.

Could I hit the brakes with cruise control on? I couldn't remember.

We left the car behind quickly, but it didn't leave my mind. I kept my eyes on the road but turned my mouth towards Grandpa Mack. "Should we have stopped?"

His head moved from the corner of my eye, but I couldn't tell if he had nodded or shaken it. He sucked in air, a sure sign he was thinking. "What fer, sweetheart?"

"It's desert on either side and mountains here. If someone was in that car, they probably need help."

"They've gotten help iffen they need 'et. They ain't been signaling fer us."

I veered around another turn and I jabbed at the cruise control, adjusting it from 60 mph to 57 mph so every turn wouldn't be a roller coaster ride.

I took a deep breath. "You're sure?" My voice twinged with uncertainty as I glanced at Grandpa Mack again. *I'd feel better if I had just stopped to check.*

Grandpa Mack patted my knee. "Trust yer Lord."

Before we could emerge from the mountain pass, we drove into a nightmare.

The rocky outcroppings on either side of the road had engaged in a gradual lowering, drawing nearer to the height of the car with each twist and turn of the road.

Without warning, the cliff faces caught fire.

Only ten feet above us, clouds of black smoke rose alongside molten red flames.

We rounded the next bend to find that the road ahead opened up into the desert. Towers of flame licked the sand between tumbleweeds.

It was like a flood of fire, devouring everything in sight.

The California wildfires.

I almost thought I'd fallen asleep at the wheel...or dreamed my sister's wedding and this whole trip. The flames didn't look real, more like cartoon drawings of fire. But a blast of heat hit the RV as the flames leapt from one side of the mountain to the other overhead.

Ashes sprayed the windshield like bullets, and soot coated the air.

The heat, stronger than the mid-morning sun reflecting from acres of desert and magnified by the windshield of the RV, jolted me into action.

I sucked in a panicked breath as a second ceiling of flame passed overhead and the metal frame of the RV groaned and protested the sudden temperature change.

"Hit the gas!" someone screamed.

Grandpa Mack had lowered his head and folded his wrinkled hands, but he stopped praying to quietly tell me, "Don't ya panic. Just keep drivin'. It's far above. Ya can accelerate without worryin' 'bout gas sparks." His gentle, rhythmic tone kept me on course. Ava's shrieks of panic echoed in the backseat.

I didn't know how to turn off the cruise control! Could I press the gas harder with it on??

Xavier's voice sounded right behind me, controlled but loud and authoritative. "We need to escape."

"Sit yerself down!" Grandpa Mack raised his voice. "Buckle up folks!" He lowered his voice and leaned towards me. "Look fer an exit."

"How do I turn off the cruise control?" I whispered, my voice tight enough to cut wire.

"Press the gas." Even Grandpa Mack's words rushed me now. I gripped the steering wheel with all my might and hit the gas pedal. We lurched forward as chunks of debris crashed onto the windshield.

"Jest keep driving, sweetheart," Grandpa Mack said.

I flinched as each piece of black-gray ash hit the windshield, barreling towards me from the cliffs above like pieces of gravel thrown on the playground.

The road curved and I barreled along the curve at breakneck speeds, the RV groaning as I reached 82 mph. I revved the engine, watching the flames creep lower on the cliff face as we emerged from the mountain pass.

Flames no longer crackled overhead, but the long curving road stretched another mile before I could see the seas of flame parted by an exit.

Flames danced all around the highway, but only dared to near the actual road at a few spots. Unfortunately the exit was one of these spots.

Flames cackled as they crisped the grove of trees adjacent to the exit. The first sign, the one 100 yards before the actual exit, said "Needles—Exit 139." We'd passed into California somewhere in the middle of those mountains.

I slowed as we approached the off-ramp. The sign that should have read "Needles" with an arrow towards the off-ramp was now a crumpled warped piece of metal on the top of two crisp sticks.

Twelve inches past the white paint a line of fire spread from one side of the off-ramp to the other. A few tongues of flame licked out onto the actual highway. We were almost there, our rattletrap of an RV chugging along at 45 mph as I hesitated. I looked to Grandpa Mack.

He watched the wildfire intently, his hands open in prayer. The light of the fires painted his face a strange orange, and suddenly his eyebrows lifted. “Go now!” he cried. “Thirty-five miles per hour. Jest reach the other side.”

I hit the brake, lurching to a slower speed as we crossed the last ten feet of space before the lane opened up into the off-ramp and the wall of flame just beyond. “Don’t we need the dial?!” My voice screeched, raised above the noise of the roaring, crackling cackling *rumbling* flames. A crack split across the top right corner of the windshield. I shrieked, swerving dangerously close to the side of the road.

Grandpa Mack’s fingers were already switching the floating dial to a random slice as he yelled hoarsely, “Go, Lauren, go now!”

I drove straight into the wall of flame on the off-ramp. *God please save us.*

I closed my eyes.

All the sounds that I’d been tuning out for the last ten minutes poured in. Fire crackling. Ava’s coughing pierced by screams. Xavier roaring directions.

The swell of fire grew distant.

I heard a sound like water.

I felt the RV still moving, grains of steering wheel material crumbling under my sweaty palms, and then I felt Grandpa Mack’s hand clamp over mine.

I jerked open my eyes.

Cars surrounded me, a truck beside me, a SUV with its blinker on in front of me.

Construction cones covered the highway to our left, the sky a beautiful pale blue with white fluffy clouds and the air pouring in from the AC smelling nothing like smoke.

Grandpa reached over me and steered the RV as the off-ramp curved left.

I stared in amazement. Everything was GREEN here. Green green grass lining the side of the road, green green trees tall and flowering in abundance with branches stretching high to the skies, and these were just in the strip of grass between the highway and off-ramp. We were in a city now.

I peered at the floating quodesh dial. The abbreviation on the slice the arrow pointed to read "AR."

"Where...on planet earth have you taken me and how?" Ava asked, voice high and tight, like a clenched fist.

"Arkansas," Grandpa Mack answered, calm as a cucumber again. He straightened the steering wheel, and my hands limply followed his lead as the wheel turned.

He held his left hand over my right one on the steering wheel with a firm, gentle grip. His simple wedding band rubbed my thumb.

My nose burned with smoke from the fire.

The fire I'd just driven into like a portal to this beautiful new world.

"Lauren, press them brakes," Grandpa Mack said as though nothing had happened. "Stoplight jest ahead."

I obeyed, actually focusing my eyes on the road and in front of me. I checked the camera, waking up from my trance. This had been nothing like the times I'd practiced quodeshing with Grandpa Mack at home.

"Turn on yer blinker," Grandpa Mack said.

I obeyed each instruction as it came and soon we were speeding down a road adjacent to the highway at 45 mph. I stayed in the right lane, a wide shoulder to my right and faster cars hurrying by on my left. It was 10:32 according to the digital clock blinking at me from the dashboard. A decent amount of traffic passed us considering it wasn't even lunch time yet.

“Well now. We’ll try quodeshing back,” Grandpa Mack announced to the vehicle as he removed his hand from the steering wheel.

A chorus of voices burst from the couches behind us. Chittering monkey laughter from Ava, sharp demands from Xavier, and unevenly paced questions from Hazel.

Grandpa Mack twisted in his seat, making placating gestures with his hands. “Settle yer horses, folks. We’ll get ta’ California.”

My hands shook on the steering wheel. Shivers ran from my core to the tips of my fingers and toes, like seizures underneath a volcano full of fiery molten lava.

Hazel’s sentiment from earlier floated back into my head, “she’s brave.”

The wildfires had restarted. They’d be part of Suzannah’s adult life.

She was brave.

I shoved my right blinker on. I glanced at the rearview camera and tapped my brakes.

Then I pulled onto the shoulder of the road, narrowly avoiding half of the tire peels littering it, my teeth jerking and chattering as we rolled over the rest.

My shoulders shook as I finally lurched to a stop. The RV engine made gurgling sounds as I turned the key to the “off” position. “I’m done.”

"WHAT JUST HAPPENED?" Ava demanded.

She and Xavier and Hazel all crowded into the driver's area. I could feel them lined up behind me, but I didn't turn. I stared at the road ahead, shaking.

My phone buzzed four or five times in a row. I squeezed my knuckles whiter on the steering wheel.

"You drive." I raised my voice to silence Xavier's boasts about how he had understood what was happening the whole time.

I removed my clenched hands from the steering wheel and placed them in my lap.

Grandpa Mack shook his head, narrowing his eyes at me in a squinty sort of way. "Thet's not the plan."

"I don't care. I can't do this." I held my hand over the scrape on my right arm from the tree back in the parking lot of that gas station in Arizona. It stung now, angry red and raised on my skin.

"I can drive," Hazel volunteered.

"You can't," I said between chattering teeth. "It has to be a...quodesher...behind the wheel."

Hazel placed a hand on my shoulder.

Her fingers were cold.

Xavier pushed himself into the space between me and Grandpa Mack. "Did you take us into the desert without water? The sink doesn't work." Each word poked like a hot brand. "My girlfriend needs fresh water. To clear smoke from her lungs." He said it as if the smoke in her lungs was our fault, for being the quodeshers and all.

Grandpa Mack nodded. "Check 'er fridge."

They went to the fridge, Ava falling into another coughing fit on the way.

I stared straight ahead.

A jagged line cut across the windshield five inches to the left of the rearview mirror and wound itself into the far corner. In that corner several smaller cracks jutted from the weak spot that had cracked from the heat. It looked like a mountain range.

I pulled the lever for window wiper fluid. Two streams of blue liquid spat onto the ash-spotted windshield and the wipers went to work.

"What's true?" Grandpa Mack asked, like a doctor offering a lollipop after the checkup.

Alright, I'd be placated. I'd act like an adult. I took a shaky breath. "We're safe," I said. "We made it out."

"Thank our Lord." Grandpa Mack bowed his head and nodded. He moved heavily, his motions bigger than you'd expect.

Most of the ash vaporized on the windshield as the wiper fluid worked. But a few flakes caught in the gouge across the windshield, smudging a layer of gray into the gap.

I marveled at the sunlight still streaming from the sky. But a faint whiff of smoke ruined the moment. My nose burned.

Grandpa Mack sniffed too and after a moment he turned the dial to increase the flow of fresh air from Arkansas to replace the stale smoky stuff from California. "We oughtta go," he said. "Wildfire ain't been everyplace. Maybe 'nother exit's safe."

I sighed. As scary as driving felt, I didn't want to tell Grandpa Mack no.

Disappointing him would be like disappointing my father and mother all rolled into one.

I turned the key in the ignition. Other drivers swished past at throttling speeds, nobody daring to rubberneck the ash-covered RV on the shoulder of the road.

"Buckle yer seatbelts, folks!" Grandpa Mack called out.

Hazel squeezed my shoulder and disappeared. A moment later, I heard a click from the backseat.

I hunched over the steering wheel, turned on the left blinker, and waited for an opening.

We followed Frontage Road until it reached its end without hitting any on-ramps. At the dead end, a black arrow painted on a yellow sign pointed to the left. "Road Unsafe When Under Water," it read.

A tree with budding pink flowers and full green leaves backed the sign.

"Turn 'er left." Grandpa Mack's voice was hoarse. He grabbed a plastic water bottle from the pocket in the passenger door of the RV.

I turned left.

I found myself choked up too—most of the smoke had gotten into the back of the RV and now it cycled through the driver's area as the AC pumped it out. My eyes watered for a variety of reasons.

Without comment, Grandpa Mack handed the open bottle to me. I drank, one eye still on the road and one hand still on the steering wheel. We drove under the highway—a simple suspended slab above us.

I handed Grandpa Mack the empty bottle. He capped it and grabbed a second bottle from his secret stash. He offered it to me.

I shook my head. The water had helped my nerves...my hands stopped shaking. But I didn't feel like drowning in it.

We made another left and found an on-ramp to get on the highway.

I drove up the on-ramp and merged.

Everything sparkled emerald green around this patch of highway. Brown brick bridges crossed overhead as we sped along at 60 mph.

It looked like we'd found our way into Oz...if only my hands weren't shaking again.

I turned on my blinker when we reached an exit, but Grandpa Mack held out a hand. "Not yet." He nodded to the sign, which said 139B. "We took 139 in California. Yer looking fer 'nother number."

Back into that wall of flame, driving into it for real this time. I suppressed a shudder. "I don't know if I can do this."

We passed another highway overpass arching above our heads, this one covered in graffiti. I didn't know what the word meant, but it had been painted in thin black letters lined with neon green, for some local gang, I guessed.

Cranes and other construction vehicles filled the median ahead, separated from both sides of the highway by poetic cement barriers and red-orange cones.

The next exit sign read: "Exit 140, Downtown Little Rock EXIT ONLY."

Grandpa Mack shook his head.

We drove in tense silence for the next twenty minutes. When we reached exit number 120, Grandpa Mack nodded.

He turned the quodesh dial a few clicks to the purple space marked "CA." It shimmered, almost see-through, like a thin coat of floating glitter covered the dial. "Yer turn ta discern."

"I can't." An iron hardness entered my voice.

Grandpa Mack nodded, his mouth falling downward at the corners. But he bowed his head and clasped his hands.

I switched on the right blinker and pressed harder against the gas pedal.

Grandpa Mack wanted me to ask God for the right speed because he thought it would better prepare me for college. That's why he had me driving.

I grit my teeth.

I had planned to catch up on those assignments in the backseat while we drove to California. That would prepare me for college much better than driving ever could.

I didn't even know how many assignments I needed to catch up on, but there was no way I could meet the deadlines now. When we arrived at the hotel in San Diego, I needed to shower before the rehearsal dinner at five. I'd probably get stuck hand-lettering wedding programs until midnight.

If I had time before the wedding tomorrow, I could turn them in late, but I wasn't even sure if I could do that. I'd turned in assignments a few minutes before the midnight deadlines, or even a few hours, but never two days late.

Grandpa Mack's brow wrinkled as he unclasped his hands. "Holy Spirit said fifteen miles per hour."

My eyebrows hitched along with my heartbeat. "What?!"

"Fifteen miles per hour," he repeated. "Yer fine. There's space fer slowin'." He gestured at the right-hand lane that had opened up into the off-ramp.

I tapped the break, signaling to the Mini Cooper behind me that I was about to slow way way down. I hit the break like staccato notes, dropping the speed, but still going 35 mph as we neared the point where the exit branched off from the highway, where the change would happen.

The air in front of us started to shimmer and I slammed the break like I needed to stop to avoid rear-ending someone.

I couldn't see California ahead of us, but I recognized that we were about to teleport, and I sure didn't want to be going faster than Grandpa Mack told me I should when we did.

The air shimmered like heat waves rising up from the road, creating a mirage without the mirage. Instead of an image of water, the heat waves just shimmered, making the actual road ahead of us in Arkansas look almost false. Like it wasn't really there.

But it was, even though we weren't about to drive on it.

We hit the shimmering spot going 16 mph. It felt like a breath of cool air.

I braked gently as we emerged. As the driver, I couldn't tell when my front tires hit the California highway or left the Little Rock highway.

The road felt the same, only our surroundings weren't. I never could catch the moment when everything changed, but I could always feel it.

We emerged to find more flames.

Grandpa Mack's directions swapped volume and urgency, like a radio station switching channels directly in my ear. "Reverse, reverse...back up! There ya go."

I slammed the brakes. We all jerked forward.

I backed up, moving the rattling RV past the line marking the highway from the off-ramp until the RV stood completely on the highway. Fires roared around us like some apocalyptic movie I shouldn't be watching before bedtime.

"Any speed." Grandpa Mack flipped the dial to another state. "Jest any speed's fine. I heard 'im. Go now!"

I hit the gas, unable to see the shimmering in the air because of the smoke. I coughed.

This time we emerged to more trees and a smacking humidity.

It felt different from the fire only in the fact that it was smokeless, because the warm, humid air clung to us like soot.

And ding! Ding! Ding! All the warning lights on the dashboard turned on, a million symbols I didn't recognize. The steering wheel shuddered under my fingers, clanking and rumbling noises roaring from the engine as loud as the fire had been a moment ago.

I turned on my hazard lights and veered over to the side of the road again. We all bumped and bounced in our seats as more lights turned on in the RV.

Smoke started pouring from the engine in white billowing clouds.

We lost power steering and I couldn't turn the wheel. I screamed and hit the brakes. Finally, we shuddered to a stop.

NO ONE SAID A WORD as smoke continued to billow from the engine. A gust of wind blew smoke through the vents and into the RV. It smelled different than the fire smoke...less like wood and danger and more like plastic and engine grease.

Grandpa clasped my shoulder, his wedding band heavy and solid against my skin.

The touch of cool metal unlocked a memory and pictures filled my mind. Shivering in a cold metal chair. A blur of emotions like the colors of a stained glass window melting. Suzannah sobbing as they asked her questions.

I snapped back to reality.

It was silent in the RV. We all sat there and stared at the smoke billowing in the breeze.

The quiet *ping, ping, ping* of liquid dripping onto metal emanated from some unseen spot in the engine.

It was like a stupor had fallen over all of us...not unlike the daze you live in after someone important to you dies.

Grandpa Mack cleared his throat. "Well now. Looks like a good time for you kids to grab some lunch."

Hazel's voice shook. "Now?"

I unbuckled my seatbelt, my head spinning as I turned around.

Xavier stretched his arms over his head as if he'd just woken from a nap. "Great. Let's grab grub for the road."

Ava giggled nervously. "I see a Subway at that gas station." She pointed at a gas station on the surface street just off the highway. We'd need to cross a weedy green field and a road with no crosswalks to get there.

The Subway sign reached high above the roof of the gas station, a lighthouse beacon beckoning us closer.

Grandpa Mack fiddled with the radio knobs, his eyebrows compressing as he lowered his ear right next to the speakers. "Go on. I'll take care of 'er."

Hazel hurried to the far end of the RV. She pulled the last of her blue Gatorade and a brown paper bag from the mini fridge built into the kitchenette.

Xavier slipped his wallet into his pocket, eyes flicking to Grandpa Mack. I could see his curiosity veering towards the boiling point the same way a car veers off the highway.

I pulled my purse from where it rested between the middle console and the driver's seat, and it felt like I was moving through water.

As I descended the steps, the radio blared. "Wildfires spreading from Route Sixty-Six to..." the announcer said, fading as my feet touched solid ground.

I coughed on smoke fumes and spun in a little circle to see all around. Little yellow flowers dotted the swath of knee-high weeds.

It looked like the RV had fishtailed towards the side of the road, because the end stuck out into the off-ramp. Cars swerved around it as they passed, sending smoke clouds drifting in their wake.

My phone buzzed.

I pulled it from my bag and read all the texts from my sister that I'd missed. Most of them were pictures of wedding preparations, but the latest one was an actual message.

Suzannah

It's a shame that you're not here yet.
At least tell me you're close right now.

Me

We're on our way.

How is Mrs. Thatcher?

Suzannah

Oh, she's fine. Where are you?

I didn't even know what state we were in. I coughed as a billow of the gray-white smoke spun in my direction. The rest of the "young folks" joined me outside the RV.

"I think that Seligman is dead and we're stranded," Ava said as we waded across the sea of prickly weeds.

"Does anyone know what state we're in?" I asked.

Ava gave me a sideways glance. "You were the one in the front seat where you could see the dial..." she trailed off, waving her hands as she searched for the right word, "...doohickey."

I glanced at Hazel, who also shook her head.

"Look-ee at this grass," Xavier drawled. "We're in the South."

We reached the road and everyone else looked for an opening in traffic while I tapped the Google Maps icon on my phone.

The address for the wedding venue showed as my last search.

My heart beat-beat-beat in my chest.

Suzannah's mother-in-law almost had a stroke today...or maybe did *have a stroke today, and all she wants to talk about is my ETA?*

I pressed the blue dot to center in on my location, then zoomed out in hopes of finding the state name.

We crossed the road and Ava yelled, "the first one to reach the Subway gets free food!"

She and Xavier raced across the parking lot.

I looked at Hazel.

She looked back, uncertain. "Who pays?"

"Probably the last one there."

Hazel shrugged like she was loosening a weight from her shoulders. "I'm not playing. My paycheck's not here. Yet."

"Still think you'll have enough?" I asked.

Hazel had been saving for a car all summer. Her face lit up as she walked closer to me, bumping my shoulder. "Hope so!"

I sighed. "We're leaving for Colorado in just under a month."

Emotions spun across Hazel's face, too fast for me to read.

I opened the tinted glass door to the gas station.

Pink cowboy hats hung on a rack in front of us. Past that and a case of glass figures, we found the Subway counter.

Xavier and Ava stood arguing in front of a startled employee at the cash register—some teenage guy with bushy hair and bushier eyebrows.

"No sweat, babe. I'm buying for us," Xavier was saying.

"Did. You. Let. Me. Win?" Ava slapped her hands together to punctuate each word, almost like she was clapping.

Xavier waved his hand in the air, his leather wallet pressed between his fingers. “Why do you care?”

Ava crossed her arms. “Listen to me, *buddy,* it doesn’t count if you let me win.”

I shot a wide-eyed glance at Hazel.

She stared at the Gatorade bottle in her hand, her face frozen in a grimace.

The employee at the cash register mumbled something and excused himself.

I followed suit, grabbing Hazel’s wrist and dragging her to a table in the corner of the store, by the windows and far away from Ava and Xavier’s yammering.

We sat and I leaned an elbow against the table, crumbs sticking to my sweaty flesh.

“Wish I was brave,” Hazel said. She opened her brown paper bag and fished out a sandwich, an apple, a bag of chips, and a homemade brownie.

It felt like a game of Jenga to shift my words into what I wanted to say without toppling the tower, but I finally opened my mouth. “Suzannah is the bravest person I know.”

Hazel’s eyes flew up to meet mine.

“She’s lived through a lot more than we have...” I struggled to get the words out. It felt like I was edging a weight-bearing block from the tower inch by inch. “But...you’re brave too.”

The statement hung in the air for a moment.

Hazel swallowed. She stared at the brown paper bag on the table, shaking her head. “The proof is in the pudding.”

Xavier and Ava invaded our table with their sandwiches just then. They were laughing.

Ava sat beside me, trapping me against the window.

Xavier dragged a chair next to her and straddled it. He locked eyes with me. "Spill the tea. He's your biological Grandpa?"

Annoyance fluttered through me. "Hot today, isn't it?" I commented, my tone bare.

Xavier turned to Hazel. "So is he?"

Hazel shrugged.

Xavier's eyes bugged out of his head. "Do you know?"

Hazel paused to answer before biting into her apple. "Nope."

"What? Isn't that girl code?" Xavier's throat bobbed like he was holding a secret and that secret was a frog inside his throat, trying to jump out.

Hazel opened her chip bag. "Nope."

I caught her eye and nodded.

Xavier clasped his hand around Ava's hand resting on the table, turning to face her. "Well, I never!" he said with an accent sickeningly similar to Grandpa Mack's.

"Well, I never," Ava repeated in a mocking Southern accent.

I unlocked my phone again.

Suzannah had sent me a huge frowny face.

I switched back to Google Maps so I could tell her what state we were in. Somewhere in the middle of the US, it looked like. I scrolled around some more...Nashville was nearby. I couldn't remember what state that was in until I finally found it in little blue letters: Tennessee.

"Tow truck's here," Hazel announced.

My head jerked up like a jack in the box. Out the window, I saw a tow truck backing up to the RV. Grandpa Mack stood next to it, waving his hands to give the driver directions.

The tow truck was huge, with a red cab and silver truck bed.

I decided not to call Grandpa Mack and ask for his lunch order.

Instead, I went to the counter and got two turkey sandwiches and a couple bags of boring chips. I knew he liked chocolate chip cookies, so I got three of those.

"I'm sticky," Hazel said, pulling the collar of her Beatles shirt away from her neck as I sat down again.

"It's a dry heat," Ava and I chorused in unison.

We looked at each other and laughed.

I'd forgotten how much time Ava and I used to spend together. Back before she and Suzannah graduated high school three years ago.

Xavier fiddled with the wrapper of his sandwich and took a big bite, paying no mind to our laughter.

For some reason, all us girls kept giggling.

I wished Suzannah was there to share it with. I pulled out my phone to text her, but then my stomach growled.

I opened a bag of chips and dug in, licking the salt from my fingers and admiring the wildflowers outside as Grandpa Mack and the tow truck driver did their thing.

"IT'S HERE!" Hazel cried.

She held her phone in her left hand and twisted it towards me, the sunlight from the gas station windows glinting off the screen.

My mouth full of sandwich, I peered at her phone screen. It showed her paycheck amount for the last two weeks at Chick-fil-A.

"It's *my pleasure* to announce I have enough saved for a Highlander!"

I squealed and threw open my arms to hug her.

Grandpa Mack arrived, lugging suitcases and dress bags. He grunted as he set them down on the polished Subway floor. "I'm 'fraid Seligman's kaput."

"Kaput?" I asked, my heartbeat echoing the word. "How will we get to the wedding? What happened? What will we do now?"

Grandpa Mack squeezed past Ava to place a hand on my head. "Calm yerself, sweetheart.'"

Xavier slapped his hands down on the tabletop. "We'll buy

plane tickets."

Hazel almost choked on her sip of Gatorade and squeezed the bottle in a death grip as she sputtered. "That's expensive."

"Sucks to be you," Xavier said.

Grandpa Mack cleared his throat. "Jest a minute. Yer not leavin' anybody stranded. We're rentin' a vehicle."

I took deep, deep breaths, but my brain boiled like hot butter on the surface of the sun. Hazel returned to slow sips of her Gatorade. Xavier and Ava hunched over Xavier's phone.

Grandpa Mack stroked my hair once or twice before lifting his hand. "Do ya fine young folks see yer belongings?" he asked, pointing a wrinkled hand at the pile of luggage.

Xavier glanced up from his phone, and his gaze sharpened. He stood and looked over the suitcases, clutching a black one with a leather suitcase tag. A mountain range embossed on the front of the tag glowered below the words, "Adventure Is Out There!"

"Lauren, ya check them hangers."

I counted the hangers. Five, one for each person there. Two suits and three dresses. I also spotted my little magenta suitcase by his right foot.

Ava and Hazel confirmed their suitcases were in the bunch and Grandpa Mack moseyed outside to talk to the towering man driving the tow truck.

I watched them talking, Grandpa in his faded yellow button-up and the man wearing coveralls and a dirty cotton undershirt. He looked like he should be barefoot, but he sported Nikes.

The second toasty turkey sandwich and two bags of chips and one extra special chocolate chip cookie crowded the table in front of me.

I dug into my second cookie as my stomach rumbled. The cookie crumbled, almost stale but still delicious.

As I finished licking the crumbs from my fingers, the tow truck driver pulled the RV onto the highway, leaving us stranded at a gas station with no transportation and the ring for a wedding that was far far away.

My phone buzzed.

Suzannah

Tell me where you are right now.

She'd also sent a pouting picture. My sister was like a 100-volt lightbulb—a megawatt smile when joy filled her features and pitch black when it didn't. There's no halfway with a light switch.

The picture only showed her top half, long and stretched out, like her limbs had been pulled out on a taffy stretcher. She wore a dangerously low-cut black tank top that somehow still covered her with a semblance of modesty. Moles covered her pale arms like red constellations.

Hair draped past her shoulders in curling-iron-created waves. She had a thin face and high cheekbones. Slightly burnt red velvet cake eyebrows framed her lashes.

Her hair was much redder than mine...she favored our father.

We both used the same redhead shampoo, designed to pull out the highlights in anyone's hair, but she'd had much better results. I was still glad she'd convinced me to try it.

Next she sent a picture of Dennis, her fiancé.

He had a strong jaw, strong nose, strong eyebrows. He'd always looked like a good brother-in-law to me.

Short brown hair crisscrossed over his forehead, cut slightly shorter around his ears. Brown moles trickled down one side of his face. Blue-green eyes full of the ocean spoke poetry on either side of his nose. He usually stayed clean-shaven, with only a few stray hairs sprouting like dots of ink on his chin.

In this picture Dennis had had no idea he was being captured by a camera. His expression, steady and straight, made me think he was talking to a caterer or florist.

He wore a black t-shirt and a red flannel, like he did most of the time. I couldn't understand how he did it in the California heat.

He joked about being fire-resistant because if the California wildfires did catch up with him, he had more layers of fabric between his skin and clothes than most people.

He seemed good at putting out fires to me, steadying my sister like a surge protector.

I knew girls usually planned most of the wedding, but Dennis had pulled his full weight with this one. He knew exactly what my sister wanted, and he did it without any fuss or flailing.

I think Suzannah admired his efficiency as much as she admired his face.

He'd proposed only a few months ago.

They were supposed to wait and marry after graduation, but when Dennis' mom had had her first stroke a month and a half ago, everyone had agreed to move up the wedding so that she could be there.

Suzannah's "oh she's fine" response to my text asking about Mrs. Thatcher might not be telling the whole story. If the ambulance had rescued her from an almost-stroke that morning, she might still be in the hospital.

"Lauren." Hazel interrupted my thoughts and I realized I'd been staring at the ceiling as I chewed my sandwich.

I made eye contact.

"Uber's here."

"What? We can't Uber all the way to California."

Hazel cocked her head at me. She had a little tan from working in the drive through. When she smiled, it didn't move her face much, but you could see it was genuine. Her ears poked through her pixie haircut like branches through the leaves of a bush. She tucked her hair behind her ears on both sides at the same time.

"Drive?" She lowered her voice, as if Xavier and Ava cared to eavesdrop in the middle of their argument about who would carry whose bags. "We need to quodesh."

"But a quodesher needs to be the one driving. Uber still won't work."

Hazel's eyes lit up and then darkened and then lit up again. "I'll buy my car!"

"Really?"

Hazel laughed. "I've waited forever."

I grinned, her enthusiasm contagious. Grandpa Mack herded us all to the Uber like a rooster gathering its chicks. I handed Grandpa Mack the lunch I'd bought for him as I piled into the backseat of the Subaru.

"Thank ya, sweetheart." There was something in his words, something that made me question if he knew what was going to happen next...and if I would like it.

Grandpa Mack sat in the front seat next to the driver—a big, tattooed guy.

The driver looked like a mountain next to Grandpa Mack's wrinkled form in the passenger seat. As all the car doors shut, the hill told the mountain to take us to the nearest rental car place.

"Sir, yes sir," the mountain said, his voice light-footed for a mountain's voice. Maybe he had a military background...his words were clipped but mild.

"Stop. New destination." Hazel leaned forward, her seatbelt snapping taut next to me. "I'm buying my car."

Grandpa Mack paused, the wrinkles over his forehead deepening. "Well now. Thet's fine," he said. "Take 'er to the nearest dealership."

"Honda or Toyota, sir?"

Hazel fiddled with her Gatorade bottle, running her fingers over the ridges along the side of the cap. "Um, Toyota?"

The driver shifted into gear with a nod.

"How are we gonna get to the wedding?" I asked Grandpa Mack.

Xavier interrupted breezily. "Can we reach California? Not at this rate."

"Wait, which state are we visiting anyway?" Ava asked, her cheeks pink as always. It kinda made you wonder if she polished them, like waxing apples every morning.

Nobody answered her. It was silent, the driver glancing at his passengers for a moment of confused consternation.

"We're in Tennessee," I finally volunteered.

Ava bobbed her head in a nod.

"Y'all going to a wedding?" the driver piped up. His Southern listlessness merged with his perkiness like coffee and cream mixing.

"Yes indeed," Grandpa Mack answered.

"When?"

My stomach squeezed as I answered him. "It's in San Diego. Tomorrow."

He swiped another look at us all as he navigated surface streets. "Yes, ma'am." He returned his eyes to the road.

A muscle along his jaw twitched once, twice, three times. He inhaled. "Would you like to reroute to the airport, sir? Nashville International's thirty minutes away."

Grandpa Mack shook his head. "No thank ya."

The driver nodded, the circular tattoo on his neck rippling like waves. Tension ratcheted up a notch in the vehicle.

Xavier leaned forward, gripping the headrest of my seat. It jerked sideways as he pulled. "But we can reach it by Sunday, right?"

The driver raised an eyebrow. "Driving?"

"Sunday?" I asked.

"I don't care if we miss some wedding. I'm just going to watch this pretty girl catch the bouquet, but if we miss our cruise boat..." he trailed off, pulling his hand away from my headrest and clenching his fists.

I turned around to glare at him in the backseat. "That's my sister's wedding you're talking about."

"It doesn't look like we can make it to either one, does it?" Xavier snarled. "We need to turn around and go to the airport like he said."

I shook my head. "Grandpa Mack can *quodesh*. We don't have to worry about getting to California. Hazel is buying us a brand-new car—thank you, Hazel—so there's *no problem* getting to my sister's wedding on time."

I inhaled, blood rushing to my head.

Xavier grinned at me, his arm tightening around Ava's shoulder in the backseat. "There is a problem." His teeth glistened. "We don't know what exits are safe to quodesh on, do we?"

The silence between us crackled like fire.

Like a sword clanging, the Uber driver piped up with a one-word question. "Quodeshing?"

We tried to explain, but he didn't believe a word we said. When he pulled up to the dealership, he rubbed a hand against the back of his neck, revealing the mermaid tattoo on his forearm. "Sorry to interfere, sir. You're...miscalculating. Allow me to drive you to the airport?"

He waited with bated breath.

Grandpa Mack shook his head. “Thanks fer your concern.”

The driver released a gusty sigh and dropped his hand to the steering wheel. “Don’t give up the ship,” he said. And he drove away.

"YOU KNOW WHAT I'LL DO FOR YOU? You know what—I'll throw in the floor mats too. No charge." The car salesman pointed at the contract on his desk.

My phone buzzed. Another text from my sister.

Suzannah

Grandpa Mack told me the whole story

Me

Yeah...

Suzannah

Me

It's okay. We'll make it.

Suzannah

It's a shame

As Grandpa Mack and the salesman kept bargaining, Hazel shifted in her seat. We'd been at the dealership for like, three hours.

The sales guy, literally named John Smith, had tried to make conversation the whole time. He asked questions we didn't want to answer again and again, like a wind chime spinning in circles and always playing the same tune.

Ava and Xavier guarding our pile of luggage had made quite the impression. Even after they'd moved outside instead of sitting in the lobby like dragons guarding their hoard.

Grandpa Mack had even made good on his threat to walk out and go to another dealership once, because a second dealership was right next door.

We were a caravan with no van, and Grandpa Mack said that was like a guarantee that they'd overcharge us...unless we showed that we wouldn't stand for it.

Hazel really wanted a Toyota though, so we'd come back.

Since Hazel called him Grandpa Mack like I did, how we were all related seemed inconspicuous...you know, unless you were John Smith, car salesman.

He kept sneaking glances at me.

We all sat in the office with the wide windows and the sales smell and the cheap cushy chairs. The office had swallowed us in one gulp, just like a monster under the bed.

John Smith slid the contract across his black modern desk. "Certified Used Vehicle—you can't go wrong."

Grandpa Mack pulled his reading glasses from the pocket of his shirt and unfolded them.

I returned to texting.

Me

I was driving. 

Suzannah

he didn't tell me that. are you okay??

Me

Yeah.

I'm so glad to be on solid ground though.

Suzannah

BET.

Me

Hazel is buying her first car rn.

Suzannah

how long before you pull in the driveway???

I didn't know how to respond to that, so I tuned back into the dealmaking.

Grandpa Mack sniffed once as he flipped a page of the contract. His sharp intake of air almost came as a snort. He scanned the next page, and I watched Hazel watching him.

She looked more pale than happy and excited. Sweat flecks sparkled on the left side of her face and neck.

My legs ached. I stood in the corner because they only had two customer chairs.

Maybe that's why I seemed like such a tagalong to the car salesman...

John Smith sat with one leg propped on the other, leaning back in the special salesman chair, comfy and confident.

Grandpa Mack had pulled his chair right up next to the desk as he pored over the papers. He tried to flip to the next page and grabbed the corner unsuccessfully two or three times before he licked his pointer finger and peeled it like a banana.

Hazel sat like a kid in the dentist's chair: fists clenched, jaw tight, her whole form upright in anticipation, although her feet only barely touched the floor.

Hazel was my tiny friend. She was also my closest friend other than Miss Eunice. Both of them I wanted to tuck under my arms and hold sometimes, even though they were too spunky for that.

For all her 5'1" frame, Hazel was the kind of person I figured God would give the ability to fly in heaven.

I could just imagine pure white wings spreading from her back and carrying her into the sky. Wings that suited her like the falcon's wings fit the falcon. She wasn't bouncy, but she had some sort of grit that I couldn't place and didn't know where it came from.

I only noticed her shortness when she was scared, like now.

Grandpa flipped to the last page of the document.

I saw him lower his reading glasses to peek at Hazel. His clearing his throat and settling back into reading was the only outward sign that anything had changed, but after he finished the contract, he folded his reading glasses and looked up at John Smith. "Ya folks sell cigarette adapters? Fer charging phones?"

John Smith's "seal the deal" smile faded. "Yeah—yeah we do," he clapped his hands once, "but I can't throw one more thing in. This deal's a *major* bargain!"

Grandpa Mack stood, contract in hands. "Thank ya. We'll jest mosey round and find ya iffen we decide we want 'er." He waved the papers in his hands.

"No—no, I've got five—*ten* other customers interested." He grinned and pointed at the phone on his desk. "One call—you're out of luck! I don't want you to miss this deal—so let's wrap it up and sign now."

Hazel stood, her shoulder blades straightjacket tight.

I tucked my phone into the pocket of my black athletic shorts. My heart beat-beat-beat in my chest again—I didn't want to spend three more hours at this car dealership. We needed to reach San Diego so I could hole up in a hotel room or something and pound those assignments to pulp.

I sucked in a breath.

Through the window, deep tones of robin's-egg blue in the sky seemed to call me out to play. The wonder of treetops in every direction still knocked me off my feet.

Shades of green shone like jewels on a pallet, emerald green and army green and light leafy green and umbrella green and dark sulky green all present in the canopy of leaves.

I noticed a glint of light on the desk as I passed. I traced it back to the gigantic silver watch on John Smith's wrist. A work of wrought metal and winking glass, it reflected the sun onto the black desk and jittered as he moved.

John Smith leaned back in his chair as we left. "Your loss!" he called.

Grandpa Mack led us away from the offices and through a hallway with a car in the middle of it, sun glazing across the windshield. "What do ya think?" he asked Hazel after a moment.

"Um...how much?" she asked.

"The number ya said. Iffen it were only the car. But they added extr'ee fees."

"Total?" Hazel's voice wavered.

Grandpa Mack showed her the paperwork.

Hazel's eyes widened. "I can't." She paused, her eyes dropping for a moment. Then she straightened her spine and raised her head. "I'm paying cash."

My stomach turned.

Grandpa Mack's bushy eyebrows pulled together. "Do ya like 'er?"

She'd been less than enthusiastic on the test drive, but I couldn't tell if it had been because of John Smith's awkward questions or the car itself.

Hazel bit her bottom lip. It was chapped and I realized my Chap-Stick was still in the RV that had been towed to a car-fixing place.

She bobbed her head up and down like the horses on a carousal ride. "Yes."

Grandpa Mack placed a hand on her shoulder. "I'll cover extr'ee fees and the gas money."

Hazel took a step back. "I..."

"Ya can and ya will."

I grinned. Grandpa Mack made everything so much easier.

He reached out a hand and dropped it on my shoulder too, so a "young folk" stood at the end of the length of each arm.

He switched his gaze between my face and Hazel's as he finished. "Yer doin' a service. Yer bringing Lauren ta the wedding."

Just me? What about him?

I studied Grandpa Mack's wrinkles, his tufts of Einstein hair, his salt and pepper beard jutting over his collar, the jovial twinkle in his eyes. But underneath the twinkle, I still sensed sadness.

The sadness in his eyes was an unpopped bubble, floating on the breeze, too high for a toddler to poke with her chubby fingers.

The contract in his right hand pressed against my back until he dropped his hands from our shoulders. “The Lord’ll always provide. Well now. Do ya have questions before ya sign?” He waved the contract in his hand.

Hazel shook her head. “As long as it’s paid upfront.” Eyes wide, she followed him as the guest of honor follows the waiter to a table spread with delicacies.

He found the cigarette adapters, bought one, gave it to her, and then led us back to the office where John Smith waited with a slick grin.

Hazel signed the papers with a still-shocked flourish.

John Smith procured two pairs of keys and tossed one to Hazel and one to Grandpa Mack.

Grandpa Mack snatched his from the air with one hand and a slight frown beneath his bushy beard.

“You’re driving off with a brand-new car—don’t forget the floor mats and the spare tire! *I* keep my word.” John Smith tucked a hand in his pocket, strolling to a back door in the room. “Ashley—Ashley! Put the tire and floor mats in there before they pull it around.”

“Already accomplished, sir,” a voice squeaked from the back room.

“Good—good.” John Smith flipped back towards us like a card in a magic trick. “Let me escort you to the car. It’s waiting.” John Smith wiggled his eyebrows at Hazel. “Can’t wait to drive away in your first car—huh?”

Hazel bobbed her head.

“Sixteenth birthday present?” John Smith asked Grandpa Mack.

Grandpa Mack hid a smile. “Graduation.”

John Smith’s eyes shot back to Hazel. “You’re headed to college?”

“I’m eighteen.”

John Smith glanced from her to me.

Hazel had short, decaying-leaf colored hair.

I had reddish brown hair, long and tangly. I was also handful of inches taller and less tan...we really looked like nothing more than friends.

If Suzannah had been with us instead, John Smith car salesman would've had no trouble. Her hair was even redder and she was even taller, but you could still pick us out in a crowd as being likely to belong to each other.

Hazel dropped behind the adults to walk with me, cupping the keys in her outstretched hand. A flimsy laminated yellow tag, long and rectangular, stated that this here car was a Toyota Highlander, Certified Used Vehicle, white.

"What's his problem?" she whispered.

I glanced at John Smith, car salesman. "Nobody ever told him that curiosity killed the cat."

She snorted.

Outside, right by the shiny white car, Xavier and Ava stood with our pile of suitcases.

It was a very normal car. It looked like a station wagon maybe, or a box on wheels. Very upright, with no slants to curve down the mouth of the hood or soften the transition between seats and trunk. It felt unassuming, like the car was plain and knew it and liked it, as if it was saying, "I'm vanilla—deal with it."

Hazel grabbed at my arm, her eyes fixed on the gleaming hood.

"That's my car," she whispered.

We pushed through the double doors, the air outside hitting us like a wet washcloth.

"Is this it, are we finally ready to start traveling again?" Ava asked as soon as she saw us. Her pink-apple cheeks shone with sweat, and she'd pulled her curls up with a clip. "I'm tired of sitting on this boring old sidewalk."

I nodded. We'd all need to shower before the rehearsal dinner... and the seconds were ticking down.

"WHERE'S THE LOCAL QUODESH EQUIPPER?" Xavier challenged Grandpa Mack.

John Smith, car salesman, stopped his slow retreat to the door of the dealership. His ears perked up like he'd heard a dog whistle.

He glanced from me to Hazel to Ava to Xavier to Grandpa Mack to our luggage and back to Grandpa Mack. His eyes narrowed. "Are you leading these kids?" Without waiting for an answer he continued, addressing us now: "Quodeshing is—it's crazy, it's not real, he'll put you on drugs or hypnotize you. Don't go—stay here and I'll protect you." John Smith, car salesman, puffed up his chest.

He faced Grandpa Mack, both of his arms spread out as if he shielded something special instead of the glass walls of the car dealership behind him.

Grandpa Mack stood, arms at his sides, wild white hair cockeyed and an innocent twinkle in his blue blue eyes. "All them young folks know iffen quodeshin's true. They're welcome ta leave any time."

When none of us moved to hide behind his barrier, John Smith, car salesman, took three brisk steps to the sliding glass doors. "I'm calling the police!" he yelled on his way in.

Grandpa Mack patted the hood of Hazel's new car with a *thunk-thunk* as the metal in his wedding ring resounded against the metal of the hood. "Good question, Xavier," he said as if he hadn't been called a cult leader less than three seconds ago. "*We're* them quodeshin' equippers."

"What the—why did you take it?!" Xavier burst out, clenching his fists.

Grandpa Mack shook his head. "Ain't worth fightin'. Lord can prove himself. Iffen he wants to."

Hazel unlocked the doors to her shiny Highlander. "Um, will the police come?"

Grandpa Mack sighed. "Not many believe. Not in quodeshin'. Call 'em prank calls."

"I can prove it to them," Xavier growled. "When the officers come, I'll shove them in the car and—"

"We'll be long gone," Grandpa Mack interrupted. "Iffen he calls 'em. First, we need yer quodeshing dial. It's simple ta git. We jest pray." Grandpa Mack placed his left hand on the hood of the car again, the white spreading underneath his knuckles like blinding sand on a beach. "Hazel, it's yer car."

Hazel placed her hand on the hood, her keys still clutched between her fingers.

I remembered the last time we'd prayed for a quodeshing dial in a car—the dial had sprung up like a flower sprouting in fast motion.

Grandpa Mack turned his head to make eye contact with me. "Lauren, lead 'er."

Oh no. I drew my hands from the pockets of my shorts and planted them on the hood between Grandpa Mack's hand on my left and Hazel's hand on my right.

Grandpa Mack scanned Xavier and Ava's faces over my head. "Y'all are welcome ta join." Then he nodded at me.

I almost hoped he could see the unease swimming in my eyes like a goldfish in a bowl. "Dear God...please let this car quodesh." I squeezed my eyes closed. "I ask this, um, in faith. Amen."

Then Hazel and Grandpa Mack prayed.

I pried open my eyes. The place above the dashboard had started to glow.

A shimmering grew on the other side of the windshield, white and bright-hot, then tendrils of color sprouted from the spot on the dashboard where the dust gathers as a car grows old.

Gasps emerged from Ava and Hazel as the dial finished forming and Grandpa Mack clasped a hand around my shoulder. "Well done," he whispered in my ear.

"I'm not comin' with ya," Grandpa Mack said after we had loaded our suitcases and garment bags into the back of the Highlander.

Grandpa Mack separated a hanger from the rest of the garment bags and draped it over his arm like he was playing waiter. "I'll Uber ta the shop. Where they hauled the—rather, *Seligman*—an' figure the situation. Young folks drive the car. Search fer any exit number under ten. Thet'll bring ya straight into San Diego on I-5. I don't want ya to risk quodeshin' on any higher number."

Xavier and Ava and Hazel gathered around like kids waiting for a fight on the playground.

"But what about you?" I cried. "You need to be at the rehearsal dinner too."

Grandpa Mack set his suitcase on the ground and grasped my shoulder. "I know how ta hand over a bride. I done it before."

Grandpa Mack pulled the ring case from his shirt pocket and cradled it between his palm and fingers as he offered it out. "Ya lead, Lauren." He glanced around the group.

Xavier was motioning with his eyebrows to his girlfriend, who didn't see it. Her eyes were fixed on the ring case in Grandpa Mack's outstretched hand.

Hazel drummed her fingers against the side of her car, jaw set. Her eyes looked like the ground had come up to meet her, like when you fall from the monkey bars and realize the playground turf isn't so far below.

"Get 'em there fer the wedding," Grandpa Mack continued. "Deliver this ta yer sister." He pressed the ring case into my hand. Soft black velvet tickled my skin.

I shuffled my feet on the smooth pavement of the parking lot. "Are you sure about this?"

Grandpa Mack stuck me with a steady look. "What's true?"

"I'm...not a leader," I said. My voice jumped like a fish in that wind up catch the fish game.

Air whistled through Grandpa Mack's nose as he inhaled. "Not *yet.*"

I grasped the ring case with white knuckles, my voice small. "But what if I don't have any leadership potential?"

Grandpa Mack patted my shoulder, his worn wrinkles like leather against my skin. "Thet's not true. I been training you fer life."

A shiny black car pulled up to the curb ten feet ahead of Hazel's Highlander. Grandpa Mack handed Hazel the second pair of keys to her car and started walking towards the new arrival. "I'll fly iffen it's needed. See ya in San Diego!"

I ran after him, my feet pattering across the pavement.

He stopped for me and I rushed him with a hug. "I love you, Grandpa Mack."

"Love ya too, sweetheart," he whispered into my hair. A thin strand of sadness wrapped around his voice and vibrated in my gut.

"I won't let you down," I whispered.

And he got in the car with a wave to us all and the shiny black Uber zipped away.

I watched the tires whirl and the car jerk to a stop at the stop sign and then turn right and speed away. We were alone.

I turned around to find the others looking at me. I almost cried.

How could I be the leader? These people were older than me, all except Hazel.

"What on earth will we do without a proper adult?" Ava asked.

I walked around them to the trunk of the Highlander and slammed the door shut, securing our luggage inside. "We drive to California."

XAVIER AND AVA CLAIMED the backseats for cuddling, so I headed for the passenger seat.

I needed to be as far away from them as I could if I wanted to focus on any of my economics assignments.

I still didn't know why I chose economics...aside from that it was math and sounded like a fun summer class. But economics—college economics especially—felt as impossible as saying goodbye to a loved one.

I beelined for the door while reaching for the phone in my pocket. I could access my student portal from there.

I welcomed the opportunity to dig into the assignments. I couldn't think too hard about leadership...or leaving Grandpa Mack...without the risk of falling apart.

Maybe it wouldn't be so hard, because we had really easy instructions. Find exit number ten, quodesh straight to San Diego, and then the rehearsal dinner.

But the sinking feeling in my chest, my stomach, my heart, and my soul told me otherwise.

Hazel appeared around the front of the car, and I realized I'd been standing there with my hand on the door handle for a while.

She held out her hand, fingers clenched around something bulky. I extended my own hand and she dropped something into it.

It was the keys, yellow tag and all, that John Smith had tossed at her in the dealership. "What? Why are you giving me this? It's your car." I shoved them back at her.

Hazel pushed them towards me, her eyes a fire in the lantern of her face. "Quodeshing."

A sinking feeling crept into the pit of my stomach. *Oh yeah.*

Hazel reached for the passenger door handle. I edged out of her way like a wooden doll.

She climbed aboard and the door slammed shut with finality.

Only I stood outside now, the sidewalk leading to the door of the dealership the only thing bearing the weight of my panicked stare. Through the windows of the building, I saw the form of John Smith, still watching.

Flecks of sweat beaded on my forehead. I had to ask God to do something that seemed magical and impossible to most people.

In a flash, I didn't believe in quodeshing anymore, I didn't even know if God was good or even existed.

Who was he? Why should I trust him?

I inhaled, the whole world whirring and waiting on the pin drop of my exhale.

It was like a thunderclap. My shoulders relaxed as a breeze cooled my forehead sweat. I couldn't agree with John Smith over there. I knew what was true.

I rounded the hood of the car, rubbing the yellow tag on the key ring.

No chance I could finish any of those assignments now.

I'll fail my first college class and then I'll be behind before I've even started and it will go on my transcript. And the summer drop-by date has already passed.

The key in my hand was surprisingly light, like a children's toy. I finally climbed into the driver's seat and the new car smell hit me hard.

The quodesh dial in the Highlander was different, the colors lighter, almost pastel. Yellows decorated the states I could see, and the dial pointed at "TN."

Tennessee.

I tucked the ring case inside my purse and set it at my feet, pressed the start button so Google Maps would direct us to the nearest highway, and turned the key in the ignition.

My hands trembled. My mind filled with memories of searing heat. Flames licking nearer and nearer like dragon tongues; opening my eyes to find I'd been driving with them closed in Little Rock; the RV shaking and shuddering under my grip, losing the ability to steer...

Every image flashed in my mind with intense detail, and I winced as I put the car in gear and inched it forward.

Xavier grabbed the headrest of the driver's seat and hauled himself forwards. "*He's* giving away your sister? Why isn't your dad?"

I glanced in the rearview mirror. Ava's cheeks glowed especially pink, her eyes fixed on me like a kid expecting candy.

My eyes jerked back to the road, then the dashboard. But the place where the rearview camera had been in Seligman had only radio dials here.

I took a deep breath. This wasn't the RV.

The RV had broken down, but even though this car wasn't brand new, the engine had been replaced and tuned up and certified by the car dealership, like John Smith had said. There was no danger of it breaking down.

I turned on my blinker and pulled to an abrupt stop underneath a tree. "I need to adjust the mirrors," I said. I tweaked the rearview mirror until I could see the row of trees stretching backwards as it lined the dealership parking lot.

"Did you hear our question?" Xavier asked. He was like a mosquito in my ear. I couldn't wait to find a way to San Diego.

I snapped the blinker on again and merged onto the empty road. "I did."

Xavier leaned back in his seat, his right arm stretching around Ava's shoulder.

"Turn right onto Pleasant Way," the Google Maps lady told me. I turned on my blinker and waited for a car on the main road to pass.

"But are you gonna answer?" Xavier pressed.

"Nope," Hazel answered for me. She pulled the cigarette adapter from a plastic bag proclaiming "Nashville Toyota South." Then she dropped the rumble-jumble, crumply-crinkly handful of plastic grocery bag onto the floor underneath her seat.

I turned onto the road, awaiting my next direction from the phone lady.

"He said 'I know how ta hand over brides,' right?"

I nodded tightly. We were nearing the highway.

"And he said 'I done it...'" Xavier tried again, his voice grating in my ears. He waited for me to finish the sentence.

When I didn't, he continued. "'I done it before,' right?"

Hazel wrenched around in her seat. "Stop it!"

I merged safely onto the highway, my heart thump-thumping like someone was chasing me.

A grin tickled the corners of Xavier's mouth. He pulled something from his pocket and a second later the slow clicking returned.

Click. Cliiiiick.

Ava caught my eye in the mirror. "I'm so incredibly hot I'm melting, and we haven't seen anything cool on this whole trip. We should quodesh to someplace nicer."

Sweat trickled down my back like a snake, sweet-toothed and smacking. I considered. Cool air sounded so nice right now, but was that what God had given us this power for? I figured it was for helping other people, not ourselves.

We passed the first exit off-ramp and I gripped the steering wheel, continuing straight.

And anyway, the whole thing made me nervous. My hands had just stopped trembling on the steering wheel. "Sorry. We just need to find exit number ten."

Cliiiiick. "But in California we can't cool off, right? Isn't it better to reach it fresh?" Xavier grinned, his charm falling flat. A bird trying to spread its wings and faceplanting in the grass.

I grit my teeth. Like he cared about my sister's wedding. "We just passed exit number one hundred and fifty. We're driving until we hit number ten."

Cliiiiick. CLICK.

Xavier leaned his body into the front seat, pen hidden from sight. "Wow, are the numbers rising? We need to take this exit and turn around."

I turned on my blinker, checking over my shoulder to see if I could get off here.

"Stop!" Hazel reached for my hand on the steering wheel, a warning motion. "He's lying." Her mouth dropped in fascinated horror as she turned to Xavier. "You planned to...turn the dial. Without permission!"

Xavier just shrugged and returned to the backseat.

My jaw dropped. Fear and anger were two blades on the pair of scissors cutting my tongue loose. "Do you have any idea what that would do, Xavier? If we quodeshed and I wasn't driving at the right speed, we would crash—we'd rear-end the person in front of us or be hit by the person behind us. You almost just caused an accident." I glared at him in the mirror.

He looked back coolly. A kid caught with his fist in the candy jar. "Huh, isn't your quodeshing safe?"

"Not exactly," I said. "God puts us a safe following distance behind the car in front of us going from the actual highway to the exit and the car behind us, but we still have to be going the right speed!"

"The right speed, huh? How do *you* know it?"

I gulped. "It's a—discernment thing." Somehow he had nailed my problem on the head. "Ask the Holy Spirit an' listen," Grandpa Mack had told me a million times. "Trust him to guide ya right."

My problem wasn't that I didn't trust God, it was that I didn't trust myself.

"What do you mean?" Xavier asked. The pen cliiiiicked.

Hazel had stopped fiddling with the packaging on the cigarette adapter, listening. A quick glance in the rearview mirror showed Ava listening too, and a tailgater behind us.

I hit the gas pedal harder. The Highlander plowed ahead, much more responsive than the old RV. The rails marking the side of the highway sped past with ricocheting speed. "How am I supposed to explain something in a couple of minutes that took me years to learn?"

"Stop stop stop!" Xavier yelled. He pointed at the window like a boy aiming a toy gun at a target. "Pull over."

I slammed the brakes, jerking to the side of the road. The tailgater narrowly missed us, swerving and honking into the next lane.

I bit my lip, breathing hard, wind rushing from my nose. Another car passed, also veering into the left lane to avoid us.

I twisted around in my seat, my heart thump-thumping. "Xavier, what in the world?"

He was climbing across his girlfriend's lap, his torso blocking my view of her face. He reached for the door handle and swung his feet onto the shoulder of the highway. The door slammed shut behind him.

Hazel's left hand covered her mouth, her golden purity ring hugging her finger.

Ava's hair hung limply from the clip she'd clasped to the back of her head. "Don't ask me, but it's always possible he had to puke."

We all turned like synchronized swimmers to scan the back window.

Sure enough, Xavier had moved a good distance from the Highlander and studied the grass as he went. His floppy hair hung limp from the heat almost as much as his girlfriend's.

My phone buzzed.

Suzannah

Tell me how close you are right now.

Rehearsal dinner is in 1 hour. WHERE ARE YOU

Me

Don't worry, Suze. We'll make it.

And then I looked around, taking in the West Tennessee highway that held us in its sweaty grip. The nearest exit number was 135. *Oh no.*

Another passing car rattled the Highlander with a rush of raging wind. The wind felt like a hot slap to the face.

Ava fanned herself. "I'm still so hot I'm melting—I should get out for some fresh air too."

"AC!" Hazel crowed, punching buttons and dials on the dashboard. Her happy crow was like the topmost layer of icing on a bittersweet cake.

The back passenger side door opened again and Xavier appeared, silhouetted by heat waves. He held a skateboard. He shoved it into the car ahead of him, barely missing Ava's face. "Some guy left this on the side of the road. Nice, right?"

Ava and I made eye contact, all the girls giving a collective shrug.

Xavier scowled as he crammed himself past his girlfriend. He and the skateboard dropped into the seat behind me, and I craned my neck to look at it.

It was one step above a piece of junk, with peeling grip tape and strips of smiley face duct tape strapped onto the end like streamers.

"Your brothers like skateboards, right?" He grabbed Ava's hand. "Don't they, babe?"

Ava sighed. "Jordan is incredibly obsessed with skateboards and there's no rhyme or reason to it."

Xavier sandwiched the skateboard between his knees. "I'll spruce it up. Think the guys will like it when we get home?" He gazed at Ava.

I turned around, hands at 10 and 2. "We can't just stop for everything." My voice wavered. I should've said, "Don't yell bloody murder for a dirty skateboard on the side of the road," but I continued with, "We have a wedding to get to."

Ava huffed. "Stop forcing your no-fun ideas on him...it's authoritarianism at its finest. It's about the journey and not the destination, so don't make me teach you a lesson."

I concentrated on finding an opening in the highway traffic.

Hazel glanced my way as the lecture continued.

"Does anyone know what time it is in San Diego?" I interrupted with blunt force, a tumble into conversation.

Cars kept coming at intervals where I wasn't sure if I could pull in front of them or not. My side mirror showed a parade of cars every fifty feet. Maybe I could merge between the blue hatchback and the beige minivan, or maybe I'd be crushed.

My blinker ticked, a timer counting down the seconds since I had signaled that I wanted to merge; the seconds that I'd been trying to find a path forward without being crushed.

Hello, can I merge? I imagined asking the driver of the next car. It was a long gap between the minivan and the cherry-red sports car, but the sports car was accelerating fast.

The seconds ticked down as I debated. The minivan passed us. I started to press the pedal, but with one last glance in the side mirror I stopped short.

My heart beat-beat-beat in my chest. We weren't going to make it on time.

After the red car passed us there was nothing but a semi far in the shimmering hot distance. I slammed the gas pedal to the floor.

I hadn't heard the click of Xavier reattaching a seatbelt after we stopped for his skateboard rescue and I didn't think Ava had ever worn hers in the first place. "Buckle up!" I cried with adrenaline pressing against my veins.

I shuttled the car to a full 50 mph, glancing at the semi.

Skid marks led off the road ahead and I wonder what had happened there. The dark tire lines looked like the stamp inspired by the *Cars* movies that I had used for craft projects as a little kid.

Reaching a respectable 75 mph, I loosened my death grip on the wheel.

The skies and grasses passed peacefully for a few miles. Then a sound like a plane engine filled my ears. My eye darted around and I realized that the semi had changed lanes and was now in my blind spot.

It had a white cab and truck bed covered with fabric like a covered wagon. If this semi was drawn in a *Cars* movie, it would have a strong jaw and square eyes.

I glanced at the clock, and a sinking feeling grew in my stomach. "Does anyone know if this is right?" I asked.

Hazel bent over the clock. "It's not."

"The rehearsal dinner is at six." My breathing hitched in my chest. "Suzannah texted that it's in an hour. Are we going to make it?"

Hazel tapped on her phone for a moment before she scoffed. "She's exaggerating. One hour, *fifteen minutes*."

"But we'll make it in time?"

"Here, I'll set the clock."

We had a whole argument about Daylight savings time, and what that means from our time zone to this one because Arizona doesn't observe it, and by the end I was only confused, but Hazel was certain she'd set the clock right.

I focused on driving.

Tennessee couldn't measure up to the beauty of the mountains over the desert between California and Arizona, but it had its perks.

The variety in landscape for one: although we mostly drove

through trees—huge green well-watered trees—we also saw clearings and cities and flat open spaces. We saw shoes by the side of the road, and suitcases, and a single throw pillow.

And then we saw a tall woman walking along the shoulder of the road with her thumb stuck out.

I pulled over.

"WHY ON EARTH ARE YOU STOPPING..." Ava's voice hitched higher with each word, "or wait, I probably don't want to know because it's incredibly stupid."

Xavier snorted. "You know that's a hitchhiker?"

I took a deep breath. Time for leadership. "Can't we help a hitchhiker better than anyone else? Quodeshing is for helping people."

Xavier pressed the clicker of the pen in his hand down flat. "Grow up," he said.

I snatched the pen from his hand and buried it in the space between my seat and the middle console.

Ava slapped a hand over her mouth, eyes wide.

Hazel cleared her throat. "We need to keep moving."

"But she's stranded!"

Her mouth set in an uncertain line. "It's not the time, Lauren."

"If not now, when?"

The hitchhiker had spotted us. Her long hair was mousy brown and curly, her skin too pale for sunshine like this. A backpack rested on her shoulders.

I hovered my finger over the button to roll down the passenger-side window as she neared. "And it's a girl, so she probably won't hurt us," I said. "She's outnumbered anyway."

Murmurs of protest rose from every side.

I pressed the button and silence fell.

The woman stood six feet back, fidgeting. She spoke when the window had finished rolling down. "Uh—uh—y'all headed towards Indianapolis?" Her voice would've tasted like a stale bank sucker if I'd unwrapped it and put it in my mouth.

"Yes!" I replied, my tone perky to cover up that I had no idea where that was.

"Bless your heart." The words dropped from the woman's mouth like a sigh. Her eyes flickered to the backseat. "I, uh—my family lives in Indianapolis."

"Xavier, on your life switch seats with me this instant, Xavier, or I swear, I'll..." Ava whispered in the back.

A single, "babe," accompanied the rustle of clothes and clank of skateboard wheels behind me.

The woman made eye contact again, her brown eyes wide. "Uh—uh—can I hitch a ride?"

"Yes." I smiled, friendly-like.

Her eyes darted all around for a moment, like she expected some monster to emerge from the woods behind her. Then her lips curled upward in a weary smile. The words came out heavier than the smile. "Thank y'all. Thank y'all ever so much."

She swung the backpack from her back, opened the door to the backseat, and plunged inside.

I leaned over the middle console to whisper in Hazel's ear. "Where's Indianapolis?"

The woman wore mom jeans and a gray t-shirt. She stank.

I tried not to cough on the fumes, but to be honest it was hard to believe an odor like that could come from a human.

"This is a bad idea," Hazel whispered under her breath. Her eyes darted towards the backseat. "We're on a time limit."

"My mom—"

"I know."

"If someone had helped her, maybe she would've made it." I straightened, grasping the steering wheel with both hands.

Hazel leaned farther across the center console. "Listen, I think we might be late for the rehearsal as is."

I quirked an eyebrow at her.

"One mile a minute, one hundred sixteen miles to go. Plus bathroom breaks."

I tucked a strand of reddish hair behind my ear.

Hazel sighed. "That's a little over two hours."

My heart beat-beat-beat in my chest. "I guess she'll have to find someone else to hand letter the programs then."

"You're—" Her eyebrows lowered.

"Since when is Suze in control of my life?" I hissed. "Maybe we'll miss it, but we'll be on time for the wedding, so what does it matter?"

"The wedding *is* the real deal." She bit her lip. "And we can't make it to the rehearsal dinner either way..."

Finally, she pointed her chin at the dial. "Indiana," she said.

We both straightened in our seats and turned around.

The woman was nodding at something Ava had said, but after a moment fixed her attention on us.

"I'm Lauren." I extended a hand.

She took it and rubbed her sweaty palm against mine. "I'm Nicole Barnes—uh—uh—sorry it's Daft." To the lead-coated silence she added, "I'm a baby's-butt-new divorcee."

"It's nice to meet you, Nicole." I smiled. "We're gonna get to Indianapolis really fast."

She sucked in air. "Uh—uh—what—uh—do you mean?"

"Well, we're quodeshers," I said. "Have you...heard of it?"

Nicole shook her head like she wanted to shake my words out of her ears. "I know about that—I know about that. I-I-I—God shouldn't give that power."

I froze, awkward silence descending on the car.

I removed my hands from the steering wheel. I didn't want it to look like I might start driving at any second, whether Nicole wanted to hitchhike a ride in this car or not.

Xavier piped up, his words breathy. "But you'll reach Indianapolis, right?"

Nicole looked from him to me. "Uh—uh—uh," she stuttered, "uh—so where are y'all headed?"

"We're going to California for my sister's wedding."

Nicole's eyes darted around the car. "Why y'all in Tennessee then? Can't y'all—uh—uh—go wherever?"

Ava smiled, her apple blossom cheeks shining pink in the sunlight. "The journey is always more important than the destination, because we get to enjoy all parts of the country...maybe even Hawaii."

Nicole peered at Ava while she talked, then locked eyes with me again. "How—uh—how much—uh—jumping will it take?"

Her hand landed on the door handle. "I don't wanna put y'all out none. I've no need for Hawaii."

"We're not going to Hawaii," I said to Ava's corner of the car.

Then I inclined my head in Nicole's direction, extending a tendril of welcome like some helicopter seed spinning down from its tree. "It's just one jump. Then we'll be somewhere in Indiana."

The woman looked like she was pushing thirty, but she acted like a nervous teenager. Something fragile caught in her eyes, like a wounded wild animal. Her gaze flicked towards Xavier, the only male in the vehicle. "Y'all friends?"

No one knew how to answer that.

Hazel pointed from herself to me. "We are."

"We're all travel companions to her sister's wedding," Ava said, "on our way to deliver the ring and watch their destiny unfold. Lauren, you should show us all the ring—I've never seen it up close before."

I pulled my purse from the middle console and placed the small bag on my lap. It sported a modern pattern and multiple pockets. I had tucked the ring in the outermost pocket, the one that had a flap secured by Velcro.

I opened the special pouch and pulled the black velvet ring case from it. Cupping the lid in one hand and holding the scratchy flat surface of the base with the other, I cracked open the case and turned it towards Hazel.

Her jaw dropped as light glinted off the ring. I spun the case to show everyone else. Nicole and Ava gasped. Even Xavier raised an eyebrow.

Fourteen karat black gold formed the circlet of the ring, looking like nothing so much as vines wrapping around a tree root. In fact, actual molded vines emerged from the center of the ring and twisted out to the side to hold the kite-shaped stone in place. The stone shone white with a splash of moss green reaching into its center. Suzannah called it "moss agate."

Another black metal vine emerged from the other side of the stone. Little diamonds grew on that metal vine like fruit. The largest diamond aligned with the kite-shaped center stone, reflecting dots of light like freckles across the faces gathered around.

This ring had cost thousands. When Dennis had shown it to her, Suze had just about dropped dead.

"It had to be resized," I told them. "Because they rushed the wedding so much, Suzannah didn't have time to stay in town and pick it up before the wedding. So Grandpa Mack volunteered..." I trailed off.

Grandpa Mack had volunteered to bring the ring, the same way he had volunteered to bring Ava and Xavier and then Hazel.

Xavier nudged his girlfriend with his elbow. "Like what you see, babe?"

Ava's jaw still hung open like it was on a hinge. "That ring is one of the most incredibly beautiful things I have ever witnessed in my life." She giggled.

"When—uh—when is y'all's wedding?" Nicole asked.

"Tomorrow." I took several deep breaths. "But we can drop you off tonight if you're okay with quodeshing? It's just one jump."

"Uh—uh—go on then." Nicole straightened her shoulders. "Y'all grasshoppers won't hurt me none. I—uh—I really need the help."

My whole face lifted. This was what I was supposed to be doing—leadership for the win. Wouldn't Grandpa Mack be proud?

I put the Highlander back into drive and announced, "Here we go!"

I merged onto the calm highway, marveling at the lack of traffic. We didn't see another car for the next five minutes of driving.

When we finally reached exit number 127, I swallowed air like a baby taking its first breath, only I didn't cry and scream to test out my new lungs.

With a twinge in my belly, I turned the dial to "IL" and flipped the blinker to the right. It tick-tick-ticked.

I prayed in my head. *God, what speed should we be going on the other side?* After a moment of silence, I realized that Grandpa Mack normally addressed the Holy Spirit. Did it matter?

The off-ramp was guarded by tree sentries on either side of the road. Tall trees, like redwoods but not so unique, cast dangerous-looking shadows on the pavement as I drew closer.

The branches overhead formed a tunnel...making it look like we should be able to enter a magic portal through them. I almost expected glimmering pixie dust to fall from the leaves. We only had a few yards before we hit the line.

In my head I pleaded with God. *Please let me know! I'm relying on you to come through. I need you now.* A breath of fresh air hit my brain. The number "37" glowed for a split second in my brain like a neon sign.

I hit the break. "Please let it be God and not my imagination," I said to myself. The words were so vivid I still can't tell if I said them out loud or in my head.

Pines and the gray off-ramp shimmered in front of us. A tight tension held all us occupants of the car in a chokehold except for Hazel. She leaned forward as if she could will us to reach the line faster.

The speedometer read 45...43...40...

I tapped the break one final time before we hit the line that marked the separation between off-ramp and highway.

At first it looked like nothing had happened except for the faint glimmer on the front of the Highlander, like heat rays shimmying up and down in the air and bouncing off the white hood. I couldn't see that it had entered a new world. But then light rain hit the windshield and Hazel and I jumped. The rearview mirror showed Nicole, Xavier, and Ava still lined up in a row in the backseat. Their dry windows showed the Tennessee forest outside.

Nicole's mouth tightened and her brow furrowed and her eyes clenched shut as she gripped the backpack on her lap. Her fingers bit into the straps.

Then the rain hit them too, splashing against their windows, droplets rolling down the glass like kids in a race.

I focused on the road—the black car in front of me seemed to be going thirty-eight miles an hour and I pumped the brakes. I should've slowed down more.

We stopped at the red light ending the off-ramp. Gas stations stood to the right, food past the bridge on our left, and the highway straight ahead.

I continued on a course to remerge with the highway.

"Wait...I cannot believe it...what on earth did you drink from a second ago?!" Ava asked, part impressed and part disgusted. Her voice was like two halves of grapefruit—one gleaming perfect and the other rotten.

I peered in the rearview mirror to see Nicole holding a tube that spouted from her hiking backpack. "I-I-I—uh..."

Hazel turned around to look at it. "Hmm. Useful."

"Not really. Uh—the more water you carry, the more you lose in sweat." Her voice turned bitter. "The more you lose in sweat, the more you need to drink to keep from passing out on the side of the road."

Xavier crossed his arms. "Wow, you're homeless?"

I merged back onto the highway just then. The light drizzle seemed to have just started but none of the other drivers slowed down, even though it was hot enough outside to melt a stick of butter...or at least turn it all gooey and shiny.

Grandpa Mack had warned me over and over that when it was warm and rained in the South, the oil rose up and the roads got slick. And if I should ever choose to travel there, I'd have to be careful.

Nicole shrunk in her seat. "Y'all don't know, I—"

Road noise filled the car as she cut herself off.

When she spoke again, her words rolled slow, like a gumball spinning its track round and round the base of the gumball machine. "My ex beat me. Kicked me out, y'know? Family might put a roof over my head for a week or so." She moved a handful of her long mop of brown hair away from her twisting face. "I won't get used to it none. Sooner or later, you're fending for yourself again."

The swish of the AC blasting made the space sound like a ventilated greenhouse instead of a white Highlander zooming along at 75 mph with a solemn conversation happening inside.

"I'm so sorry," I said. "What else can we do to help?"

"Y'all are already doing plenty." Nicole shrunk closer to her backpack, wrapping her arms around it and tucking in her shoulders, making herself small on the seat.

We passed a green sign saying: "142 mi to Indianapolis."

"Shouldn't we be much closer to Indianapolis than one hundred and forty-two miles?" Ava asked. "That is an incredibly long distance and I'm feeling nauseous." Her voice sounded nasally. I glanced in the rearview mirror to see her nose scrunched against the smell emanating from our guest.

I shrugged and returned my eyes to the road. More cars crowded into the three-lane highway here than in Tennessee.

"Oh!" Hazel cried. She had leaned down to peer at the dashboard and now she pointed to the quodesh dial. "We're not in Indiana!"

WE WERE IN ILLINOIS. I'd taken us to the wrong state.

Apparently Indiana and Illinois shared a border, though. "How far is it to Indianapolis if we don't make another jump?" I asked. My hands had melded to the ridges on the underside of the steering wheel.

"Two hours. Twenty-five minutes," Hazel reported, holding my phone.

About an hour ago, she'd jolted upright in her seat. "My phone is at the car dealership!" she'd cried. She'd used my phone to call Grandpa Mack and asked if he could go back to the dealership and retrieve it for her. He'd said yes, of course.

Hazel hadn't mentioned Nicole, the new addition to our expedition, on the phone call. I wished she had. Grandpa Mack needed to know how we were using quodeshing for good!

Hazel still held my phone, the official navigator since I didn't know the difference between Illinois and Indianapolis. Apparently it was two hours and twenty-five minutes.

"We could jump again," Hazel offered.

I gripped the steering wheel tight. "I think I'll just drive."

"You sure?" Hazel pointed at the map, her eyes wide. "It's east."

Xavier groaned from the backseat. "Why are you thinking about this? Just quodesh again."

Ava shook his arm, her curls bouncing. "But Xavier, imagine how much more time we have for adventures! Think of what we can see."

"Babe, it's Illinois. We're gonna see cornfields," he said.

Nicole stayed in her wrapped-up position, her backpack the present and herself the wrapping paper clinging to it—but she nodded when I asked if we could just drive the rest of the way to Indianapolis. "Bless my stars. That's fine," she muttered into the backpack.

Hazel directed me off the highway and then onto it again.

But when we started seeing signs for the world's biggest rocking chair and wind chime and golf club ten miles later, I knew I was in trouble.

"Look here, it's not simply the largest rocking chair in the United States, but in the whole world, which we will never have another chance to see, so we should go." Ava clutched at the back of my headrest.

Before that point, I'd never realized how much power the steering wheel gave somebody. I'd always thought about the responsibility of being a driver, keeping your eyes on the road, not getting distracted no matter what happened in the backseat...

But right at that moment I realized that no matter what anybody said, I could keep driving if I wanted to.

Like when we played cops and robbers in the church basement as kids, they were my hostages. And unless they jumped out of a moving car, they would go wherever I steered.

All sobered by those realizations, I stared at the road.

"It's near dinnertime," Xavier announced, languidly taking leadership. "We need to stop for food. And gas."

I checked the gas gauge. The tank was almost empty.

We stared each other down in the rearview mirror for a moment. His pen went click...cliiiiick.

Be cool, I told myself. And I turned on the blinker.

Inside the Dairy Queen, we all stood in a clump by the front counter.

All except Hazel. She'd bought a snack pack of peanut butter crackers at the gas station and now she munched on them at the back of the group, nearest to the island with the ketchup and napkins and straws.

I edged past everyone else to stand with her.

My shoulder brushed the sleeve of her faded brown shirt as I settled into a spot where I could peruse the menu. "What are you gonna order?" I asked.

Hazel swallowed the cracker in her mouth. "I have food."

My eyes widened as I turned to face her full-on. She met my shocked glance with pink cheeks and her mouth in a firm line.

I put my hands on my hips and glared. "That's NOT enough. You need more."

Hazel shrugged and stared at her shoes.

I couldn't release her from the grip of my gaze, even as she kept her head lowered for another long moment.

When she raised her eyes, something lurked behind their cheered glaze. She held up the cracker pack as if she were making a toast. "Two bucks."

My mouth dropped open involuntarily. "Oh."

The flicker of her eyes said, "you know?"

My face confirmed it.

Hazel looked sick. "I can't afford college. I might leave—" She broke off, plucking another cracker from the pack and rolling it in her fingers. "After the first year."

My vision spun. College...without Hazel? That meant even if I didn't flunk out, I'd still be alone.

Suzannah was getting married, Grandpa Mack would be far away...Hazel was the only family I had left! And even she didn't know the truth about our parents.

I avoided her gaze as my words caught in my throat. "I'll buy you dinner."

She cringed.

"I want to." The linoleum flooring of the Dairy Queen glistened wet. "It's hardly enough."

The weight of how big the problem was and how unable we were to fix it settled between us.

So I bought Hazel's dinner and Nicole's and my own.

Nobody had rain jackets, but we ignored the storm clouds building up in the sky and the wrinkling rain.

When we left Dairy Queen, Hazel used the map on my phone to direct us to the world's largest rocking chair. The signs said: "Casey, Illinois—Big Things Small Town."

We settled in with our food across the street from the world's largest rocking chair and right next to the world's largest wind chime.

Nobody else meandered the wet streets. There was a closed cafe with outdoor seating, so after we hurried to the crazy tall wind chime and pulled the rope and read the Bible verse on a plaque nearby, Hazel and Nicole and I settled at the table to eat.

The rain was picking up, but the seating area boasted a roof. My purse rested against my thigh, the ring and my wallet and everything else in there.

Nicole sat on my right, both of us facing the rocking chair across the street, soaring way way above the heads of Xavier and Ava, who'd gone over to peer up at it.

My phone buzzed. *Buzz, buzz, buzz.*

"The rehearsal is starting," Hazel said. She flicked her gaze towards Nicole.

"I know." I sucked at my strawberry Blizzard, the cream so thick that my cheeks hurt, even though nothing came up through the red straw.

A gust of cold wind whipped across my face. *Should we leave Nicole here?*

I felt jittery, anxious to get back in the car. The sun was setting.

How could I leave her stranded here alone in the rain?

Nicole cleared her throat. "So, uh—uh—uh—y'all understand quodeshing stuff?"

I shoved a bite of hamburger in my mouth and shrugged at her question. Rain pitter-pattered along the top of the roof, the air growing thick with humidity.

"I, uh—uh—watched the—uh—dial thingy. How do y'all control it?"

I swallowed. Only two or three bites left. I could drink the Blizzard while we drove. "You don't, really. God controls it. Speaking of quodeshing, we need to get going."

Nobody moved. *Ugh. What* great *leadership, Lauren.*

"What if—uh—uh—uh—s-s-sorry—uh—what if you need somewhere specific?" Nicole slurped her soda like she hadn't had anything to drink in days.

I crumpled my burger wrapper. "It's like...let's say that you're on a highway in Tennessee at exit number ten. When you flip the quodesh dial to California, that means whatever exit you get off at, you're now going to be at that same exit number in California."

Nicole nodded, still slurping.

"But it's more complicated than that because...well, you have to know what speed you need to be going. You don't want to rear-end the person in front of you after you teleport. And God—well...he tells you what speed to be going at, but you have to practice listening so you don't hear him wrong."

Hazel shook her head. "I still don't understand. There are *multiple* highways in each state. Do you end up on a random one?"

Nicole's face flickered when Hazel spoke. She set down her drink and crossed her arms. "And—uh—uh—uh—what about other countries? Can you q-quodesh there?"

My heart beat-beat-beat in my chest. "I don't...know? They don't have highways and exits...so I guess not. Grandpa Mack...um...he's the one who's good at it."

Ava and Xavier joined us just then.

Ava dropped onto the bench across from me, holding her phone to her chest.

Xavier sat next to her, locking eyes with me. "You never got a chance to answer earlier," he said slowly. "What happened to your parents? Where are they now?"

I rolled my eyes. *This again?*

"Abandoned you too? I—uh—I-I-I—know how that feels." Nicole patted my shoulder awkwardly.

"They didn't abandon us."

Nicole studied me. "They're—uh—uh—not in j-jail...?"

Xavier slapped both hands on the table, half raising from his seat. "Yeah, jail! I hadn't thought of that."

I kept my face blank. "What does it matter? I wasn't a ward of the state, sad and alone and separated from my sister. We were raised by Grandpa Mack."

"You—you poor girls." Nicole turned big, guilty puppy eyes on me, as if she was the mom who had done the abandoning.

I stood. It had started raining harder, big plops of pure water dashing against the pavement and the giant rocking chair across the street. The wind picked up, sending the wind chime ding-ding-dinging. "We need to go," I announced. I took a few steps towards the sidewalk and where I'd parked the car a block up the street.

"But it's raining," Ava said.

I stopped under the cover of the patio roof and glanced out at the sky. Thick, dark, brackish clouds drowned out the last strands of sun. They spread across the expanse of the sky like plastic soldiers lined up for battle.

Xavier stretched his arms over his head and smirked at me. "We're staying right here. When the storm passes we'll get on the road, right?"

"No." My voice turned tight and hard. "I'm missing my sister's rehearsal dinner right now. It's getting dark. We need to go, and I don't care that your girlfriend doesn't want to get wet."

I'd thought that picking up Nicole would be my first step into adulthood. No more just doing what my family wanted...I'd go on a short little adventure.

Now I felt trapped. Everything was taking too long. My phone had stopped buzzing and—

Be cool, I told myself. *You're the leader.*

Hazel crumpled the wrapper of her sandwich and swung herself free from the table.

Xavier finished his stretch and yawned. "It's not safe to drive."

"Maybe you can't drive safely in the rain, but I can." I added a head tilt to punctuate my point and stepped out into the rain. Hazel followed.

I pulled the keys from my pocket and waved them in the air. "If you're not in the car in ten minutes, I'm leaving you stranded here," I called over my shoulder. I felt exhilarated, because for a second there I actually planned to do it.

Then my heart beat-beat-beat in my chest like a woodpecker returning to its favorite tree. What was I doing? What on earth would Grandpa Mack say if I showed up at the wedding without Xavier and Ava?

Footsteps pounded behind us.

"Last one there's a rotten egg!" Xavier yelled. His footsteps splashed against the sidewalk, where little rivulets of water had started to run into the gushing gutter. He shoved past us.

"Hey," Ava squealed. There was a splash. "My phone!"

I almost didn't turn around. When I did, I saw Nicole barrel into Ava, who had stopped dead in her tracks to stare at her phone washing away into the gutter.

I took a step towards them, my hands out as if I could stop the impact from a foot away.

"Ooof," they collided.

Ava had been angled towards the street, so Nicole only clipped her shoulder. Ava stumbled a step forward but Nicole, top-heavy with her backpack on her shoulders, kept going. Now she toppled into me.

My outstretched arms hit her in the stomach and her elbows rammed into my shoulders.

She scooted backwards, hands outstretched. My purse dangled from one of her hands. I could see the whites of her eyes.

"I-I-I'm s-so sorry." Nicole shoved my purse at me. "You forgot this."

I tucked it over my shoulder. "Thanks."

Her hands shook. "No need to keep—" She looked like a wounded animal again. "Leave me. I'm f-f-fine." Her shoulders folded in on themselves, hands grabbing for her sides, caving in on herself like a fortress with loose stones that might collapse at any moment. "I-I-I-I—I can hitchhike again."

My heart thumped in my chest. "No." I grabbed her shoulder and she went taut. "No, Nicole."

She met my eyes, her fear so tangible it felt like sparks flying.

"*No*. I'm taking you home."

And that was when the rain really started to pour from the sky, like an omen of what would happen next.

AVA SAID SHE WAS GETTING MOTION SICK, so she rode up front with me the two hours to Indianapolis. Secretly, I wondered if she faked the queasiness because of the smell coming from Nicole.

It had gotten worse. It was still sweat, I guess. But phew-wee!

It was a rancid, putrid, hopeless smell that rose from her in waves and overwhelmed my senses when I got a strong whiff of it.

The rain we'd been caught in had intensified all smells.

I'd turned the headlights on and the windshield wipers to strong speeds. The overcast sky grimaced overhead as it vented its grief.

Nicole asked about the skateboard after Xavier had fiddled with the tape in silence for a good fifteen minutes. "It's—it's—uh—it's for her siblings?"

"Yeah, she's got ten."

Nicole's mouth dropped open. "Ten! Are—are—are you Catholic?"

Ava groaned. "No, I am not and I never have been and I never will be Catholic."

While Xavier told Nicole all about the Greeson siblings, I turned to Ava. "Do you ever get tired of people treating you so different?"

Ava had rested her elbow against the window and her head on her cupped hand. She swiveled her head to look at me. "I do sometimes... what do you know about it?"

I adjusted my grip on the steering wheel, moving my hands to the bottom of the wheel instead of 10 and 2. "Because I get the same thing. It's like—yeah, my grandpa raised me, but I'm not a freak! There are worse things and I'm happy with Grandpa Mack! Why are people waiting for me to tell them some tragedy or something?"

Thump! I paid attention to the road again, because something was wrong. Had we hit something? Water sprayed out from our wheels, and we were skidding across the surface of the water. I moved the steering wheel towards the shoulder on our right. No response.

"We're hydroplaning! We're hydroplaning!" Ava screamed. She grabbed my shoulder. "Don't hit the brakes, or you'll kill us."

I pressed my Converse hard against the mat on the floor, bracing myself to keep my foot from reaching for the brakes even though I wanted to with all my might. *God please help.*

The Highlander spun towards the left lane, and it was too dark to see if any cars were near us. I yanked the steering wheel the other direction. Nothing happened. Was I about to wreck Hazel's brand-new car?

The tires regained traction with the road, and I turned the steering wheel gingerly towards our lane. The tires' grip with the road held, and we evened out in the right lane at a nice 45 mph.

I pressed the gas pedal like I was handling a newborn baby and we slowed even more.

An exit sign glistened through the rain ahead.

I pulled to the side of the road on the off-ramp and gulped in deep, deep breaths. So did everyone else, spitting out laughter in between gasps.

The downpour lessened along with my heart rate. Finally, the droplets spattering the windshield didn't set my heart to racing, so I followed the ramp and regained a spot among the cars herding to Indianapolis.

The zoom of cars around us increased in the next few minutes as we grew close to where the city sprouted from the flat Indiana ground. Pitch-black darkness had descended, making it hard to make out anything other than the clusters of lights.

"We need to go to Walmart," Xavier announced.

I jerked my head without turning around. My tone turned colder than our rain-drenched clothes. "What for?"

He smiled sweetly into the rearview mirror. "I'm buying Ava rice to dry her phone."

Ava's face lit up. "Wait, that might be perfect and actually fix it—thank you, *Xavier*." She said his name all slow and sultry and a spark passed through the car.

An overhead sign identified our lane as exit only.

I turned on my blinker and merged left, keeping my eyes on the road as Ava leaned over the center console.

I felt a tug on my headrest. Xavier, who was buckled into the seat directly behind me, had grabbed the headrest to pull his face forward to meet Ava's.

Smacking noises commenced.

I felt bad for Hazel, who'd been voted into the middle seat because she had the shortest legs. After a moment, I cleared my throat. "Can somebody get me directions to the nearest Walmart?"

Ava broke off the kiss and peeled herself away slowly, lingering over the center console with a smile on her mouth.

I risked a look in the rearview mirror.

Xavier settled back into his seat, a greedy smile lingering on his face, his eyes on Ava as she tapped on my phone.

Hazel blinked. The unreadable expression on her face puzzled me—she neither smiled nor frowned, her eyebrows raised slightly, her eyes wide but not shocked.

Nicole had paled, like she might throw up any moment.

When I finally pulled into the parking lot of a Walmart in Indianapolis, I turned the key and let it dangle from the ignition as the engine *ping, ping, ping* cooled.

I collapsed in my seat, unsure why I'd agreed to this stop. "Why don't you two go in and get the rice?" I told Ava and Xavier. They could kiss all they wanted in Walmart.

I would sit in the car and ask Hazel to help me with my homework.

She was better at math, but even more than that, I needed a moment to cool off before I started my mound of tasks.

It was late, and Suzannah would probably call me any minute. I needed backup.

"I need to go in," Hazel said in a small voice. She gripped her sling bag in one hand.

"Uh—I'm going with y'all too," Nicole added.

So we all went. Nicole and Hazel and I split apart from Ava and Xavier before we even entered the sliding glass doors of Walmart.

We headed for the candy aisle, where Hazel wanted to buy gum.

A gnawing ball of worry started to form in my stomach. Next to the "it's fine" clash of cymbals in my brain, everything inside of me felt like a middle school marching band playing two discordant songs at the same time.

Pay attention to Nicole, the thought popped into my head out of nowhere.

And then, Nicole started speaking.

"I used to live by those weights y'all," she murmured as we passed the produce section. "I-I couldn't buy anything more 'n a pound. I'd switch out apple after apple to find the right size."

I'd never used the scales in Walmart before.

They'd always felt more like decoration than anything else to me—especially the big red dial that swayed if you pressed your hand in it like Suzannah and I used to do while Grandpa Mack picked out the best bag of grapes.

When we found the candy aisle, Hazel pointed at something on a low shelf. "Pocky sticks!"

The box showed a picture of long corndog-colored snacks in the shape of really thin pretzel sticks, coated in colored paste. Banana flavored, strawberry flavored, chocolate flavored, and original, which must mean vanilla.

"Oooh, banana," Hazel said as I pulled a box from the shelf.

"It's your favorite?"

Hazel nodded, her eyes following my hands as I held the box at my side. I'd decided to buy it.

In the back of my mind, I couldn't help thinking about her secret. *What if she can't find the money to stay with me at college? What if she has to drop out?*

We started walking down the aisle, eying the other kinds of candies. Nicole trailed along, although I got the feeling she didn't want to be there.

I spotted a bag of Starbursts high on a shelf and grabbed the party-sized bag.

When I turned, they both stood there wide-eyed.

I grinned and made eye contact with Nicole. "What's your favorite Starburst flavor?"

She broke eye contact and massaged her shoe against the linoleum. "I—uh, I-I-I don't know," she mumbled.

"I like lemon," I tried again, but got no response.

"So how did you hear about Pocky?" I asked Hazel, shaking the box. "I've never seen it before."

She lowered her head. "It's Japanese."

I nodded. Walmart felt like a whole new world with Nicole and Hazel at my side. So much to explore and discover and realize about other lifestyles and cultures and people.

At the very end of the aisle, we found the gum and the peppermints all haphazardly together. Hazel gripped the strap of her sling bag, which was made of blue-and-purple flowered fabric. Her knuckles turned white as she surveyed the gum selection.

Nicole stuck her hands in the pockets of her mom jeans before staring off at the ceiling. Her wet hair hung in long, long coils down to where I guessed her belly button would be if she had been standing up straight.

Hazel grabbed a pack of fresh mint gum. "Helps motion sickness," she commented, steering us out of the aisle and towards the checkout.

We met up with Ava and Xavier at the car, where they held each other in another lip-lock.

I grabbed Hazel's arm as we reached the car. "We're not quodeshing. That means you can drive."

Her face lit up and she fished the second set of keys from the pocket of her Bermuda shorts. “Let’s go!” she cried.

Ava broke off the kiss, but Xavier didn’t release his arms around her. Ava started to pull away. He still gripped her.

Ava frowned and grabbed his arm.

Should I do something? I didn’t think I could, even if it was part of my leadership responsibilities.

Hazel unlocked the car and jumped in the driver’s seat.

Nicole had fallen behind us in the parking lot, but now she caught up and started yelling. “Don’t take it, girl. Kick him in the groin!”

Xavier jumped, startled.

Ava pushed off his chest. “Xavier,” she grunted.

He pulled her to him again, one arm around her shoulders in a protective way. “What’s the matter, babe?”

I took one step closer. “Get in the car,” I said with no force. Before I could face the results, I hurried around the Highlander and climbed into the passenger seat.

I set the Walmart bag of candy on top of the crumpled bag that had held the single cigarette adapter we’d bought at the car dealership only a few hours ago. We’d all lived a lifetime since then.

My tank top clung to my skin as I buckled my seatbelt, the fabric freckled with spots of drying rain.

I pulled my phone from my purse and stuck the charging cord emerging from the cigarette adapter into my phone like a sucker into a gaping mouth.

The back car doors opened and slammed shut. Hazel and I made eye contact.

She pointed at the phone in my hand. I opened up the map and entered in the address Nicole mumbled.

I set the phone in the center console.

"In two hundred feet, turn south onto Woodland Avenue," the map announced.

Hazel pulled out of the parking spot.

I peeked into the backseat, still using the rearview mirror because I didn't dare be that obvious. Xavier smiled faintly as he poured rice into a bowl.

Ava had her hand on his bicep.

Nicole scowled at the floor, as close to the door as she could possibly get, holding her backpack as a life preserver, keeping her afloat and away from the couple.

I yawned and checked my phone. 73% battery and it's twenty-one minutes after midnight, local time.

We'd woken and started our journey at 5 AM in Phoenix. I had no clue what the time zone difference was, but it had been a long day.

I distributed a handful of Starbursts to each person in the car.

Nicole tried to push them back into my hands. "Oh, no—uh—uh—no thank y'all." Her nostrils flared, like she was a scared animal again. "I can't—all y'all are already—uh—too kind. The ride and dinner and—uh—uh—"

I pulled my hands away. "I want you to have them."

Nicole released a nervous squeak and deposited them into the space on the seat between her and Xavier, the little pile of Starbursts a wall between them.

She looked out the window as we entered a nice neighborhood with a manicured garden bed around a sign stating the name of the neighborhood.

A pang of sympathy filled me. I couldn't imagine not knowing if you were welcome at your parents' house or not. It was awful.

I yawned, stretching my shoulders. "Alright, guys! We've put a lot of good hours in today. Let's get to exit ten and quodesh to California."

There was a thrill in my stomach as I said the words. *Quodesh...*

Hazel whipped her head towards me, then back towards the road. "Didn't you notice?" Pitch-black darkness seemed to cling to the windows of the car. "We've been going the wrong direction."

My heart stopped beating. "What?"

Hazel shrugged. "We've been going east, but the numbers go west. We're closest to exit number 205."

"No," I moaned.

She raised her eyebrows. "I thought you wanted an adventure."

"Not like this! How far away are we?"

"Two...and a half hours?"

My neck clenched stiff from so many alert hours of driving. Ava's eyelids drooped as she leaned against Xavier's shoulder.

"It's late already and it'll be even later after we meet Nicole's family," I said. "We can—"

Nicole's spine stiffened. "I—uh—I—uh—want to—uh—face them alone."

Her eyes were wide. Two faint lines ran from her nose to her cheeks, and her lips were pressed together.

"Are you sure? What if they're not home or something?" I released the words without slipping up and saying "what if they send you away?" because that's what I was really thinking.

Nicole pressed against the seat, her shoulders jumping up two inches. "No—no—thank y'all. I—uh—I'll sleep in a backyard."

A ding came from my phone and Hazel pulled us to a stop in front of a two-story stone house, all lit up with lights like they were expecting someone.

The front door was painted blue, with a welcome wreath hung on a nail. I hoped it would hold true when Nicole knocked.

The manicured lawn surrounded the cobblestone driveway with multiple cars parked in front. I wondered if one had been Nicole's back when she was learning to drive. Back before she left home for college or trade school or wherever she went. Or maybe everything had changed since she left. Maybe this wasn't even the house she grew up in.

I wasn't about to ask.

"Do or die," Nicole whispered to herself between gritted teeth. What a pep talk.

"You've got this," I said.

She gave me a dazed glare. Then she looked over at Ava half-asleep on Xavier's shoulder. She looked at Hazel with her hands on the steering wheel. She avoided my eyes as she opened the door and climbed out onto the grass guarding the sidewalk.

Hazel had parked us under a small tree, and the branches caught Nicole's tangled hair as she turned around, clutching her backpack to her stomach like it hurt.

Nicole placed her hand on top of the door. "He's bad news," she muttered in Ava's direction. "Get out while you can." And she slammed the door closed.

Ava's eyes flew open and she sat up, staring after Nicole.

"Hey!" Xavier yelled.

Nicole dodged the parked cars in the driveway. Someone was definitely home. Still clutching the backpack like it was precious, she climbed three steps to the porch and stood stock still, staring at the door.

"I'm feeling motion sick again, like I might puke at any moment," Ava announced. "I need to sit in the front."

I shrugged and slid my seatbelt free, grabbing my purse and emerging from the car into the fresh air under the tree.

Nicole startled when I left the car. I waved and walked around to my new seat.

I got in and Xavier slid over.

Hazel showed me a map to the Sleepyside Motel with a tired frown. "Can we afford one?"

Ava piped up from the passenger seat. "We need TWO hotel rooms tonight...one for the girls and one for Xavier."

Xavier leaned forward, a whiff of cologne catching me in the face now that I could sense smells other than Nicole's sweaty clothes. Water droplets dripped from Xavier's hair into the cup holders in the center console. "You're gonna send me out alone? C'mon, I could just sleep on the couch or the foot of your bed."

Ava batted her eyelashes at him, then dropped her smile like a hot coal. "No."

Xavier sighed and receded into his corner of the backseat to play games on his phone.

"Okay." I took a deep breath of Nicole's sweat and Xavier's cologne. "We need to pay for two rooms. Why not split it?"

"I can't," Hazel said helplessly.

"I bought cruise tickets last week," Xavier added.

"We could bill it to my parent's credit card and they might not notice right away," Ava offered.

I groaned.

"I INSIST." XAVIER HAD LOADED his arms with suitcases and draped the dress bags over his shoulder. One hanger tangled in his thick hair like it was grabbing on for dear life.

Ava's cheeks turned a dull red—her makeup washed away and blush drying in streaks. "If you drop the baggage, I will be incredibly upset," she said.

Her hair hung in long wet loops, strands cloistered between her silver necklaces. She stood with her feet spread apart, as if on the deck of a ship.

Hazel wrinkled her nose and closed the trunk of her car. "Air freshener," she said.

I watched the gears turn in her head as she mechanically added another item to her list of things to pay for. Her hair had suffered the least from the rain in Casey—only the curls had been washed right out of it. Now it lay flat and straight as a heavy curtain hanging from a rod.

Everyone else walked across the parking lot with an assortment of luggage while I peeked in the side mirror to see how I had fared. My hair tousled and frizzed in a playful swoop on top of my head, like it had waved to the wind and danced with the rain. Because I only wore a little makeup, my face shone with the brilliant beads of water caught in my eyelashes and clean-washed cheeks.

Hazel locked the car and it beeped.

"Which direction should we go at the moment, fearless leader?" Ava called.

I pushed away from the car and hurried to catch up, a grin flying across my face for a fleeting moment. I held the key cards, I'd procured the rooms, I'd done the leadership adulting thing. My partially dried hair whipped in the wind as I joined the others standing at the bottom of the concrete stairs.

At the top, a green roof and metal railing provided shelter, like they were cupping the walkway in their hands. "They didn't have two openings next to each other, so we're in 203 and Xavier's in 114," I said.

We mounted the stairs, Xavier leading the way with his barrage of baggage.

I felt like an ant, just the next one in a line of workers marching for their queen. And our queen would be Suzannah...the one whose wedding was dragging us halfway across the planet.

Lights were spaced along the walkway, their weary flickering the only signs of life.

The motel seemed secluded, like a jungle village in the middle of nowhere. I looked over the railing, into the darkness, and a creeping sense of isolation gripped me with cold fingernails.

Was this how my parents had felt before they died?

Xavier stopped directly in front of the door for room number 203.

I glanced back at the string of doors that we had passed. It was funny, how we'd been counting down numbers all day.

I dug in my purse until I grasped the paper cases of two key cards.

I pulled both from the bag and slid the one marked 203 in the door handle slot. After half an eternity, the light flashed green and I opened the door.

Inside it smelled like air conditioning and smoldering rain and smoky woods.

As I walked through the narrow opening between the closet and the bathroom, it grew stronger. *Is that pine?*

Walking into the room was like walking into a small cluster of trees, because there were wooden frames on the two beds and wooden accents all around. On the far wall, an AC unit underscored the blinds hanging over a huge picture window.

I was drawn to the blinds first, sliding them out of the way.

We didn't have a view of anything but the dark parking lot, where a single streetlight attempted to drive back the dark.

I shivered. *Oh well.*

The blinds clattered together like wind chimes as I shut them.

I turned to see Xavier drop the suitcases in front of a couch I hadn't noticed at first. One of those tall lamps with a dingy white shade stood next to it.

Hazel set her stuff on a rickety old wooden desk. *That's where I'll be working all night,* I thought.

Xavier flipped the dress bags from his shoulder to the first bed. Two of the bags peeled back to reveal their contents.

Both were black. Black like suits. Not like the lavender bridesmaid dresses that Ava and I needed.

"No," I cried. My eyes darted from dress bag to dress bag, tallying up the number and colors and shapes of what we had left. "Grandpa Mack took the wrong one!"

Xavier's grin split wide. "He'll have ta' hand over yer sister in that yellow button-up."

I glowered. It felt like a large fist was squeezing my chest. "So help me, we will NOT miss my sister's wedding under any circumstances." I slapped the second key card into his hand. "You're on the first floor."

He stuck it in the pocket of his shorts, grabbed the remote from the TV table, and collapsed onto the couch.

Ava and Hazel gathered around the dress bags. We spread the four outfits across the length of the bed. All we were left with were the two suits, Hazel's dress, and one bridesmaid dress.

Xavier patted the seat next to him. "Babe, come watch TV."

"I need to know whose dress is here and whose is missing." Ava reached over to read the tag. "Size twelve—this one is mine."

I scrunched my eyes closed.

"Babe!" Xavier repeated.

Ava joined him on the couch.

I thought about sliding to the floor and having a good cry. But I needed to hold it together. Everything would be okay...I just needed to focus on my assignments.

I sat at the rickety old desk in the corner. *This is great luck*, I told myself. *It's like God put the desk here just for me.*

Hazel laid across a bed with a huge sigh.

Xavier switched the channel from the news about the California wildfires to a rom-com and put his arm around Ava.

I pulled my computer from my desk and everything else turned into background noise. *Open the tab, input my password, look at the due dates in a separate tab, see how far behind I am...I have five hours of lectures to listen to and a quiz due in twenty minutes.*

I groaned softly enough that even Hazel didn't stir from the notebook she scribbled in.

My breath felt like an elusive creature in that moment. Like a fairy slipping through my grasp and flying away.

I dug in my backpack for headphones. I could guess on the quiz and risk a bad grade, or I could wait, turn it in late, and risk a bad grade.

Where were my headphones?! I thought I'd packed them last night—I remembered wading through the papers in my room at Grandpa Mack's house, surrounded by boxes because I'd been packing for college, and finally finding the headphones. I'd slipped them into the front pocket of my backpack.

So why couldn't I find them? It's not like they could have been stolen.

My phone jangled "Wake Me Up" by Avicii. I held it to my ear. "Hello?"

Grandpa Mack's homemade quilt voice came through. "Where ya at, Lauren?"

I stood, pacing towards the window. "We're in Indianapolis right now."

"Shoot. Ya can stay the night with my friends. I'll call 'em and ask fer ya, iffen it's not too late..."

"We've already got a motel, Grandpa Mack. So thank you, but it's alright."

"Alright sweetheart."

I should tell him I have assignments due and end the call. I could feel the seconds ticking down to the deadline, like a wind-up clock in my stomach.

Grandpa Mack inhaled before talking. "Well now. I ended up with a flight fer five AM ta'morrow. In-laws offered ta pick up."

I swiveled on one foot, making an about-face in my pacing. As I turned, I caught movement from the corner of my eye. Xavier had stood. Maybe he was finally leaving for his room. "That's great."

Grandpa Mack's voice nodded and I envisioned his head nodding along. "Fer me, it's a blessing. Good opportunity ta get ta know 'em."

I made another about-face, turning back towards the room. Ava still sat on the couch, peering at Xavier as he held that annoying skateboard.

Realizing I was thirsty, I beelined for the bathroom and the pasty paper cups always stacked next to the sink. "I—um, I need to go, I think..." I trailed off, a burning sensation in my chest, like I'd swallowed a spicy candy.

"Alright," Grandpa Mack said, his voice drawling into trails of Southern twang. "Jest know thet I'm on a plane tomorrow. After I land I'll look fer more safe exit numbers."

I sighed in relief. "We're at exit 205, so we should beat you to San Diego if we leave early. But thanks."

"Yer—"

My phone buzzed and banged against my ear like a fire drill alarm.

Another call, this one from Suzannah. I bit back a silent sigh. I couldn't ignore her call, not on the night before her wedding.

My voice raised unintentionally. "I need to go, Suzannah's calling me!"

I hung up, barely hearing his "goodbye sweetheart," and held the phone to my ear again.

"Hello," she said, her voice a single lightbulb hanging in a dark room. "Tell me why you've ignored my text messages."

I pushed through the door to the bathroom and my hand froze halfway to the stack of blue-and-yellow paper cups. I'd forgotten to respond to most of her text messages about the rehearsal dinner. "Um, I've been driving. What did I miss?"

"The rehearsal dinner turned out fine, but James—Dennis's best friend whose parents are hosting the wedding—wants to do a choreographed dance or something for the reception entrance. I'm like, 'Sir, please stop messing with *my* wedding.' I can't believe he's being such a diva."

"Oh I'm sorry." I'd zoned out for most of what she'd said, but that seemed like the best response.

"It's a shame, especially since it might rain tomorrow. We need the weather to cooperate and his mother to feel better all day, or at the very least not seize during the ceremony. They say big events like this can trigger more seizures and that would be awful."

I blasted water from the faucet into a paper cup. The sink looked dingy yellow with a thin line of pink around the metal drain stopper. White flecks spattered the metal surface of the faucet and its handles. I peered into the water to make sure it was at least clear.

It looked like water.

I glanced at the shower to see it ringed with pink lines all around. "Sounds good," I answered, wondering if I should try to shower before we left for the last leg of our trip or wait and do it right before the wedding.

Her voice snapped like a whip. "I need you here as soon as possible. So tell me where you are."

I gulped down air, my full cup of water untasted in my hand. "We're in Indianapolis, which is in Indiana."

"Tell me how long it will take you to get here. Will you arrive tonight?"

Ava appeared in the doorway of the bathroom, holding up her phone while she typed. Her phone case was white with hot air balloons on it.

I took a swig of water, moving into the hall.

She blocked me, waving her phone in my face. "The outlets don't work in this hotel room," she started, "the lamp won't turn on, and my phone isn't charging in any of them because nothing works."

I stared at her for a second. How was that my problem? And what was I supposed to do about it?

Suzannah spoke again, something deeper than casual conversation in her tone of voice. "We could postpone the wedding a few days. It's a shame to marry without my sister showing up."

I ignored Ava, turning towards the emergency fire escape sign posted on the inside of the door. "No! I'll be there."

"How can you be sure?" Suzannah asked. Her voice was plagued with uncertainty.

Ava tapped my shoulder. I shrugged her off and opened the door, slipping outside.

I leaned against the railing overlooking the parking lot. "Look, you can't postpone your wedding just because I'm running late. There's a lot of other people involved."

"Yes I can, Lauren, because it's *my* wedding. I don't see why I'd need to ask permission."

I jumped in. "Suzannah, I don't want you to postpone your wedding."

"Mr. Lee came in—hi, sir—so I need to go. *Promise me* you'll be here."

"I will."

Suzannah hung up and I peered at the sky. Barely distinguishable wisps of white dampened the full velvet blackness of the night. A star winked at me as the wind blew, the light moving in and out of sight. I should've hurried back to my computer, but for some reason I stopped. I stretched my arms wide, drinking in the world that God had created.

A bang shocked my arms back to my sides. Xavier burst from the motel room. He tramped past me with nothing in his hands but clenched air.

I walked back into the room. Luckily, he'd left the door open, because I'd left the keycard on the desk.

Ava stood at the end of the hallway with crossed arms and lowered eyebrows.

Hazel stared at something out of my sight with wide eyes.

I craned my neck to peer around the wall as I came closer. The lamp lay on the floor, cracks in the lampshade splintering in pieces around the spot where it had landed. Xavier's stuff still littered the thin carpet.

"I can't believe him! I can't—argh!" Ava exploded.

Hazel twisted her mouth. "You invited him."

"Did you expect me to bring someone other than my boyfriend as a plus-one?" she asked as I hurried out the door and after Xavier.

Through the balcony railing, I saw him reach the last step, his untied shoelaces yammering against the concrete.

"Hold up," I called and pointed towards the motel room with a firm finger. "You're paying for that. And set your alarm for six AM sharp."

Xavier spewed a couple obscene words and disappeared under the awning.

Back in the motel room, the blinking numbers on the little bedside table alarm clock read 1:32 AM.

I told the girls to set their alarms for six. Bridesmaids were supposed to be there at eleven.

Just as I started to settle into the first lecture video, Hazel tapped me on the shoulder. “Go to bed,” she said. “You’re driving.”

I came out of the bathroom to find Ava zipping up Xavier’s suitcase, white-faced. She gave the skateboard a swift kick, then picked up Xavier’s things and headed for the door.

She balanced the suitcase and skateboard in front of her, arms loaded and full as she entered the narrow pathway where I stood.

Hazel had already gotten into a bed, her arms on top of the sheets, pressing them tight on either side of her body. The AC unit crackled and distant shouts pierced the thin walls.

I sat on the empty side of the bed.

Hazel pressed her lips together. “If I’d started college sooner, they would’ve realized,” she said quietly. “Now it’s too late.”

A heavy, invisible weight settled on my shoulders.

Hazel stared at the motel ceiling. “The money’s gone. I’m on my own.”

The door to the room opened and shut. I had been about to say something, anything to comfort Hazel, but I closed my mouth. The scraping of the lock sounded louder than the shutting of a coffin.

Ava came into sight, her mouth straight and her posture Barbie-doll perfect. “Xavier said he will pay for the lamp out of his own pocket.” She glanced at the article still shattered on the floor. “He said he’s sorry.”

Soon after that, I tumbled into bed and turned out the lamp. Curled up all comfy-cozy with the covers touching my chin, one thought lingered in my brain.

Ava had said Xavier was sorry like she didn’t believe him, like there was some secret.

Like she knew something we didn’t.

THE SLEEPYSIDE MOTEL was not the kind of place that served a five-star breakfast. But they also weren't the kind of place that even blinked when we told them about the broken lamp. I refused to accept Xavier's offer of "paying me back," insisting that he give it straight to the motel clerk.

When we left the motel lobby, he had an armful of Little Debbie muffin pouches balanced on top of his suitcase.

"Where did you get those?" I squinted as we walked into the parking lot. The sun had gotten an earlier start to the day than us, so there weren't even sunrise colors to soften the glare.

"Huh?"

I sighed. "Where'd you get the muffins?"

Xavier dropped his head a few inches to look at the suitcase, like he was surprised to find the load in his arms. Words left his mouth in a surprised lump. "They were by the door."

"Was there a sign?"

"What's it to you?" he asked, a whine biting into his voice. His eyes were red and watery like he hadn't slept a wink all night.

What will I do if he stole them? I suppressed the flip-flopping of my heart from one side of my lungs to the other. "Because stealing is illegal," I answered with a raised eyebrow.

"Bruh, chill. They were free." He bumped me with his elbow.

I stumbled forward a step. "That doesn't mean you can take their entire stock."

"But we need at least two muffins for each person," he said, his grin broad and an unhinged glint in his red eyes. "Good leaders provide snacks."

We joined Hazel under the awning of her open trunk door. Hazel wore a red skirt with tiny white polka dots and a cute white tank top. She loaded her suitcase into the trunk. The rest of the luggage lay on the road around the rear end of the white Highlander.

I figured she'd dragged all the girls' luggage downstairs herself because Ava sat on the asphalt, leaning against a hubcap on the driver's side, her head tilted back onto the cold metal and her eyes closed.

Xavier deposited the muffins and his suitcase into Hazel's arms with a grunt before he rushed to his girlfriend.

Hazel looked down at the muffins, then at me. I sighed. The sun shone on her straight hair, bringing out hidden amber tones.

I stuffed Xavier's skateboard into the trunk.

Hazel added his suitcase to the pile. It perched on top, almost blocking the driver's view. She gathered muffins from the surface of the suitcase with a smile. "Breakfast."

I reached for the edge of the trunk door and Hazel backed out from under it. I slammed it closed with a satisfying *thunk* and pulled the keys from my pocket. "I've got to drive, sorry."

Hazel tilted her head and her ears poked through her pixie haircut like branches through the leaves of a bush.

She hurried the muffins to the front seat and I moved for the driver's door, but Xavier was blocking the way.

He knelt in front of Ava, one hand gripping her knee.

"Come on guys, we've got to get going," I said. My voice didn't shake.

Ava groaned. "We didn't go to bed until like, one AM." She groaned again, rolling her head away from us, still resting against the car. "And it's like six AM."

"That's right, babe. You need more sleep, right?" He scooped her up, Ava emitting a small shriek. When he straightened, her legs dangled over his arm and he shoved her face into his shoulder.

Her legs swayed as he moved for the motel lobby. "Want to cuddle, babe?"

I checked the time. 8:01...we hadn't gotten up at six. And then I'd wasted an hour banging on Xavier's door and dragging him to the office to pay for the lamp.

"Hey!" I yelled. "What are you doing? Get in the car!" I clenched both hands as I said it, as if condensing my fury into small balls of pulsing red light.

Xavier stopped halfway across the parking lot.

"I'm not joking. Get in the car."

Ava's head popped up from his shoulder. Her raccoon remnants of mascara and his runny red eyes both fixed on me.

But they came back and got in the car.

In the driver's seat, I blinked bleary eyes until I could focus on the weeds sprouting up from the dirt strip in front of the Highlander.

We weren't far from the highway, only a building or two away, and I could already see cars whirring along the roadways in the distance.

I plugged my phone into the cord emerging from the cigarette adapter.

"Can I check something?" Hazel's hand hovered over my phone in the center console.

"Sure." I unhooked my purse from my shoulder. "Can I put this by your feet?"

She nodded and I settled the purse in a safe spot so the ring wouldn't bounce around if I hit the brakes too hard.

I turned the key in the ignition, the plastic yellow tag tickling my hand. I switched to reverse and started to pull out.

"Stop!" Xavier yelled. "My suitcase is in the trunk, right?"

Hazel turned her head with a shocked expression, phone in hand.

"Of course it is, because you dumped it in her arms!" I raised my voice like he was the school bully. I switched to park and turned around in my seat. "What's up with the shoving people around thing?"

In the dim interior of the car, Xavier's eyes showed black smudges beneath them like he'd broken into Ava's makeup. "Nothing. I'm only checking."

"If you want to know, you can look behind you."

Xavier piped up again after I merged us onto the highway. "Another person needs to use the cigarette adapter today. It's only fair. Lauren charged her phone last, right? And the hotel outlets didn't work, right?"

Hazel shook her head, my phone still in her hand. "Lauren needs it most."

I bit back a nervous laugh...yeah. I had a wedding to attend and a promise to keep.

Xavier grumbled. "You lost *your* phone, right?"

"Xavier, Suzannah's wedding is today and she needs to be able to text her sister," Ava said, "not to mention she's the one driving, so her phone will be the one used for maps if we lose the way."

I hadn't expected Ava to stick up for me. But with all that taken care of, we cruised along. Hazel rerouted us so that it would take an hour and seventeen minutes instead of two and a half. Not sure how that worked...she just said something about exit numbers and highways.

I jumped every time my phone *pinged* until we found exit number ten.

Suzannah didn't text me at all.

"There it is, there it is!" I pointed to the exit sign and bounced in the driver's seat. That beautiful green exit sign with the big number ten and the small print saying "Two Miles" shone in the sunlight, the reflective white strips a shining path forward.

One more quodesh and I was done. "Input the address," I told Hazel. I grabbed her arm and shook it in excitement.

She laughed. "Where?"

"Grab the wedding invitation and the ring from my purse! The address is on there."

We reached the last half mile until the exit, and I could see the actual off-ramp nine yards away. The sign hung crooked, but I loved it all the same.

Hazel pulled my purse up to her lap.

I turned the quodesh dial to California. *San Diego here we come!* The dial glowed in the sunlight of a new morning, sparking like jewels.

I turned on the blinker and a huge smile stretched across my face even as I clutched the wheel with white knuckles. *Last quodesh,* I thought to myself.

The road shimmered ahead, looking jeweled too. This was it.

What speed limit? I asked silently. And I listened.

I listened so hard I didn't hear anything but a background noise when Hazel said something to me. After a moment she returned to rifling through my bag, and I focused in.

I want you to go forty-five, I heard in my head. It wasn't a picture this time, but a thought. Was it still God?

Only a few yards until we hit the line. Could I trust my hearing? My discernment? But the thought felt like a different substance than my own thoughts, or at least...I thought it did.

So I tapped the break. I had slowed to 50 mph already, so it wouldn't take long to match it. Forty-five felt fast for an off-ramp. Tempted to tap the brakes harder, hitting the line saved me from the panic. Now I'd know—either we'd rear-end someone, or be rear-ended, or everything would turn out fine.

Cool air hit my face, and a glorious sunrise streaked the sky ahead. It was like we had rewound time. I blinked and saw we were on a long looping off-ramp that spun around and wound up directly onto another highway.

"Um, Lauren?" Hazel looked sick to her stomach.

"What?" I shot my eyes back to the highway as someone honked their horn behind me. I peered in the rearview mirror. A tiny black sports car driving on the shoulder of the road had cut off a beige minivan.

It zoomed closer to us. It was gonna cut around us too.

"The ring." Hazel held up my purse, her tone tragic. "It's gone."

The black car approached and I steered us to hug one side of the shoulder, still curving around the last stretch before we lined up with the new highway. "Gone, um, gone where?"

"I don't know."

I shook my head over and over again. We were in San Diego, finally, and the wedding was in a few hours. We had to have the ring. "I put it in my purse yesterday!"

Hazel gripped my purse with both hands, her eyes darting around.

A gasp echoed from the backseat.

"I wondered if you were a dirtbag—now I know for sure!" Ava cried, shoving herself off Xavier's chest. "There's a ring in his suitcase—I found it last night!"

"Yeah, there's a ring in my suitcase," Xavier's voice turned low and tight. "Want to see it?" He wrestled his suitcase over the headrests without an answer.

I clenched my teeth and gripped the steering wheel with white hands as the black car zoomed past.

Everything that I'd surmounted—wildfires, quodeshing, missing assignments, leadership troubles...only to have *Xavier* steal the ring from me and flaunt it in my face?

What, did he think we wouldn't notice? Did he not want to attend my sister's wedding *that* badly?

I saw red, the whole road in front of me tinted with red, but not a red like the sparkling ruby red on the quodesh dial. Just a mottled rash coloring the road and the taillights of the zippy black car in front of me.

God please help me, I prayed. I blinked and my vision returned to normal.

My heart rate didn't.

I looked at Hazel—white-faced and gripping my purse as she watched the backseat. I followed her gaze in the rearview mirror for a few seconds before I needed to start thinking about merging onto the new highway.

I merged to the sound of a suitcase zipper ripping open.

In the mirror, I watched Xavier pull a black velvet ring case from his bag. He popped open the lid and showed it to Ava.

She gasped. “It’s a different ring.”

“Yeah, I know,” Xavier growled. “I noticed when I *paid* for it. When I picked it out for you, my *loyal* girlfriend.” Each of his words sounded like a punch to the gut. But they weren’t kids in a fistfight, they were adults talking about something so big as marriage.

“If you didn’t steal it, who did?” I burst out. Where on earth could it have disappeared to?

I gasped. “Nicole.” As I spit out the word, my heart dropped in my chest.

Hazel’s face confirmed my suspicions.

I turned on the blinker for the next exit and flipped the quodesh dial to “IN” for Indiana, where a certain hitchhiker resided.

AS SOON AS WE JUMPED into Indiana, my phone broke. It crashed and burnt like a toddler learning how to walk.

At least...it refused to wake up no matter how many times Hazel pressed the power button. It felt like an act of God.

"What *exactly* is your plan?" Hazel asked.

"We drive back to Nicole's house," I said. I scanned the road for landmarks.

"And then what?"

My heart beat-beat-beat in my chest. "We'll confront her." We were speeding down a one-lane highway with no median, surrounded by driveways at either side, unsure if we were moving closer to or farther away from Nicole. I moaned. "How did we get lost? We just drove this route."

Hazel rubbed her knotted forehead with one hand. "We're not in the same *place*, Lauren."

I took a deep breath.

Ava and Xavier sulked on separate sides of the backseat. After we had jumped and before I'd had time to object, Ava had unbuckled her seatbelt and scooted to Nicole's old seat. She'd grabbed the pile of Starbursts on the floor and started popping them in her mouth.

"What time is it?" I asked.

Hazel groaned. "No phones."

"No one has *any* battery, not even two percent left?" With no cars on the road, I stared into the backseat while I waited for an answer. Ava's now wrinkled and stained blue shirt looked like a blanket draped across her shoulders as she curled in the corner of the car with Starburst wrappers littered around her.

"Ava?"

She snapped from her daze and stretched slowly, oh so slowly, to a sitting position, then for the bowl of rice on the floor.

She plunged her tan hand into the rice grains. She felt around the bottom of the bowl, scowling for a moment before she found it. She pulled the phone from the rice, scattering more white granules onto the dark mats.

I checked the side and rearview mirrors for cars. Nothing. We seemed to be in the middle of nowhere on a hunt for a ring in a haystack.

Actual haystacks and fields of grass passed our windows in a charming country scene. A big, slick house full of windows smiled in the distance, glints of sunshine reflecting off the glazed-over glass.

Ava's voice sounded as dead as her phone, a touch of sharp metal needling it. "The thing is incredibly broken, it won't wake up, not even a flicker on the screen."

I nodded and gave her a sympathetic look. She broke eye contact.

There was only one other phone in this car, and no one else was going to ask him. As the leader of this fated expedition, I sucked in a breath and switched my gaze to the other side of the backseat. "Xavier?"

He snapped his head upright from where he'd been contemplating the ring case in his hands. He held the case open, stroking the velvet with his right thumb. He cast a glance in Ava's direction.

She put her nose in the air and turned away.

Xavier's suitcase had fallen to rest half-open on his legs. He didn't even seem to notice it now that it held just clothes. "Wow, you need me, right?" he said sulkily. Then he retreated into silence, staring out the window.

I returned my attention to the road. Farmhouses came closer together now, instead of the bougie bower homes.

I wanted an easy answer, a simple solution, someone to tell me what step to take. We were in the middle of nowhere Indiana, without the ring, and with no way to get it back. The sun had crept halfway up the sky already. I slammed my hand down on the steering wheel. "This should be easy!"

Hazel heaved a sigh. "Didn't you notice? We didn't land in the same place we came from. God brought us back somewhere else."

She pointed at a house on our right. There was a cross on the porch.

"Ask for directions," she said. Each word ached like a bruise.

I turned on the blinker and slammed the brakes, glad no one drove behind me on that little strip of road to nowhere. We turned onto the driveway, gravel kicked up by the tires pinging off the bottom of the engine, like tiny strikes of a hammer on a baby xylophone.

The house stood two stories tall with casement windows peeping up from underground. Painted red and white, it looked like a lighthouse. The wooden porch was covered in crosses and wind chimes. They spun at the slightest breeze and threw sounds at us like punches.

The blinds were pulled but the worn white front steps with dirt sliding across the corners seemed to call a welcome of sorts.

Xavier spoke through clenched teeth. "The last stranger stole your sister's ring. Now you want to trust another one?"

The words caught me by surprise. "Well I don't have much choice, because *you* won't let us use your phone for directions."

"Sucks to be you." He cackled until Ava looked in his direction. His shoulders hitched higher and he turned his face away, jaw working.

Hazel cracked open her door and got out, sandals crunching on the gravel as she twisted to talk back into the Highlander. "He's right." She snapped the door shut and started for the porch.

I grabbed the keys and my purse and followed.

As soon as I shut the car door, I noticed the birds. They chirped, spinning in flight above me.

My feet stuttered across the gravel to where Hazel waited on the porch steps. I stopped to shake out my legs and stretch my arms and wipe the crusts of a late night from my eyes. "Eeeeek, I'm sore," I complained.

Hazel steadied her gaze over my head, but her cheeks glistened wet. "Why'd you stop?"

My mouth dropped open. The words felt like a dam breaking, and I watched her lower her head and swipe at her tears.

The nearest car door slammed and Xavier emerged.

He walked towards us, each foot crunching the gravel and the stones flying like they were fighting back.

Ava's door opened and closed with barely a click. Even her hair sagged.

As Xavier approached, the chimes started billowing and blowing music down from the porch.

“Thanks for joining us,” I said. Slightly sarcastic leadership felt right.

He shoved his hands in his pockets and poked daggers at the gravel with his stare.

Ava passed him, gaze fixed on me and Hazel. Her eyes were as red as Xavier’s had been when he’d first thrown open the motel room door this morning after I’d pound-pound-pounded on it for at least fifteen minutes.

Her cheeks were dry, wiped clean. She tucked her hands under her armpits, the sleeves of her shirt sheltering her fingers.

Hazel and I welcomed her into our midst. We mounted the steps and approached the door together.

Xavier didn’t follow right away.

Us girls paused in front of the welcome mat, eyeing each other. The wind chimes spun, hanging from silver hooks attached to the ceiling of the porch. Bells dangling from the end of one wind chime pealed like church bells at a wedding.

Should I be the one to knock? Was that part of my leadership responsibilities?

Hazel looked from Ava to me and back again before stretching out a hand and knocking on the siding next to the screen door and underneath the white doorbell.

I pointed at the doorbell wordlessly.

Hazel reached for it as the door opened.

A lady with bobbed graying hair and an infant on her hip opened the inner door. She surveyed us for a moment before a huge smile spread across her face.

“You’ve been quodeshing, haven’t you?” The lady said in a creaky rocking-chair voice.

Hazel and I locked eyes. Alarm and awe swayed across Hazel’s face as she bit her lip.

Even Ava gasped.

The lady shushed the baby on her hip, bouncing a little. "You're not the only quodeshers in the universe, you know. But come in, come in!" She spread her free arm towards the entry behind her.

Hazel opened the screen door and stepped inside.

Ava followed, and I grabbed the door, holding it open as I glanced back at Xavier.

He sulked up the steps and shoved past me. I followed him over the threshold into a small entryway.

An itching feeling crawled underneath my skin as the screen door closed. I peered around the corner and into the living room.

Soft light filtered in through the pulled blinds. A baby blanket and toys spread across the living room floor in front of the couches. A whiff of chocolate chip cookie caught my nose, rich and warm and cinnamon-y.

I still felt like something was amiss.

The baby cooed in the lady's arms. "My name is Marge, and this is Abby," the lady said.

We all shuffled our feet in the entryway.

"I hope we didn't interrupt anything," I said.

"I'm just babysitting my granddaughter," Marge stopped to smile at the baby, "and baking some cookies." She laughed. "I can't help myself—chocolate chip cookies are what grandmothers are supposed to live for. You should take some with you, they're fresh out of the oven and cooling just now. Oh, it's not like Abby can eat much anyways. She's my first one."

An unseen fan hummed in another room.

I opened my mouth to ask directions, but Marge started chattering before I could ask.

She set the baby on the dotted pink blanket spread across the carpet. "But anyways, God gives plenty of people the gift. There's even websites out there with information about exit numbers and routes and stories to help you travel where you want to go. That is, if you want to learn that way."

"Yes ma'am," I said. "We're here to ask directions to Indianapolis."

The itching under my skin increased.

Marge patted the baby's tummy. "Oh, that's only about an hour away. My daughter lives there, actually...that's where this little one is from. Aren't you, sweetie?"

Staying silent hurt more the longer she rambled, like pressing down harder and harder on a bruise.

The way Marge talked with her hands reminded me of the professor who taught my economics class and all those missed assignments.

I could feel my GPA slipping lower by the moment. *If I want to save my grade, I need this wedding over and done with as soon as possible.*

The woman had launched into a long explanation of what the best donut shop in the city was, and I felt more frustrated with Suzannah by the moment. Words gathered in the back of my throat until they finally excused themselves from my mouth. "So, um, which direction is it?"

"Oh my—what's in Indianapolis?"

I felt Xavier stiffen behind me. Ava shot me a pained look.

This explanation could take a long time, but if I didn't answer someone else would. "Well, my sister's wedding ring is there, and we need to pick it up before the wedding."

Marge peered at me for an examining moment. "Oh, that's what you're quodeshing for?"

"Kind of. We're trying to get to San Diego and we ran into a lot of trouble along the way." My heart sank.

Hazel tucked her keys in her pocket. "How'd you know?"

"Oh, I just had a feeling," Marge said breezily. "The Holy Spirit pricking my heart, you know."

"The websites," Hazel pressed, "they teach quodeshing?"

The wrinkles in Marge's face deepened into a frown. "Oh, they all teach quodeshing, you know. How did you learn?"

Everyone else's gaze narrowed in on me. I caught the moment when Marge realized I was the only quodesher and switched her gaze to rest on my face too. I turned pink. "I learned from my grandpa. I didn't even know there were websites."

"What a wonderful legacy to pass down." She turned her face towards the baby Abby. "No one taught me. I just kind of...figured it out." She laughed. The old-fashioned pearl necklace adorning her neck bobbed as her shoulders jiggled.

I scuffed my Converse against the wooden floor below me. "We need to get going, my sister's wedding is actually in a couple hours and—wait, what time is it?"

"I'm about to start preparations for lunch," Marge responded. "Oh my, if you're not in too much of a rush, I'd love to have you join me and my husband for a meal. Albert is in the shed, I think, but he won't miss my cookies." She smiled again.

"We really can't stay...but if you could tell us how to find Indianapolis, that would be great."

Marge smiled again, her wrinkles turning up at the corners. "We could eat earlier," she offered.

I shook my head. The itching spread like hives.

"Well, let me grab some cookies for your journey and then I'll point you in the right direction," Marge said.

"You really don't—" I started.

“Wow ma’am, home-baked cookies?” Xavier interrupted, dropping his funk for a moment of manipulative charm.

Marge started for the doorway in the far corner, turned back and pointed at the baby. “Will one of you watch Abby for me? Just give her a toy and she’ll be happy.”

With that, the woman disappeared around the corner.

I wanted to chase her down and shake her until she told us how to get to Indianapolis.

Instead, I watched Ava hand a crinkly tiger toy to the baby.

The baby wore a dark pink onesie with her diaper sticking out at the edges and her bare legs topped by tiny little white socks with pink heels and toes.

She grabbed the toy in one tiny fist and shook it. But her fingers lost their grip, and she flung the toy across the room.

She screwed up her face and started to cry.

The baby kept wailing, her eyes squeezed shut tight so that she couldn’t see Ava offering the toy to her again.

Hazel had her back to me, her shoulders climbing towards her ears.

I lowered my eyes. *So she’s still upset.*

The baby wailed louder.

Xavier huffed and slid against the wall in the entryway, knocking a blue painted wooden cross crooked with his hair. He must’ve gelled it during the long interval when he’d said he was “packing” this morning, because it looked nicer than any of us girls’ hair.

The itch strengthened under my skin.

He sulked until Marge returned with cookies, then offered to carry the bag. *If cookies will stop his sulking, let him act like a three-year-old,* I thought.

Marge scooped Abby from the floor and the baby curled into the crook of her right shoulder, quieting. "That's a good girl," Marge cooed.

We all stood and watched her like robots.

"Go on, try the cookies," Marge offered.

I raised my voice over the sound of Xavier ripping the Ziplock open. "Can you, um show us the way?"

Marge put a hand to her forehead. "Oh, sorry sweetheart. I'm forgetful sometimes. You certain about leaving without lunch? Albert and Abby and I would love your company."

"We couldn't refuse, ma'am," Xavier piped up with a suave smile.

I glared at him. "I'm sorry, but we can't stay."

I grabbed the screen door and held it open, the sound of the faraway fan lessening as soon as I stepped into the midst of the wind chimes again. Everyone trooped onto the porch, covering my rudeness with their thank-yous; all except for Xavier.

He skulked past without a glance.

I shut the door and moved next to Marge, who'd positioned herself at the very peak of the steps.

"You just turn left at the road." Marge pointed back the way we'd come from with her free hand. I'd been headed in the exact wrong direction. "Stay straight for a few miles—oh five or ten—take a right on Gomber and stay there until you hit interstate sixty-five. There will be signs, you'll know it when you see it. Take that road and you'll hit Indianapolis in forty-five minutes."

"Thanks." I ducked my head. Marge leaned in for a one-armed hug, careful of Abby with her drooping eyelids.

"Oh honey, you don't have that much to thank me for." She released me and I herded everyone into the Highlander.

"Now you enjoy those cookies!" Marge called after us.

"So Grandpa Mack is your maternal grandpa?" Xavier asked as soon as all the car doors had shut.

I winced, cracking open a single eyelid to peer in the mirror.

Xavier still slouched in his seat, but a mischievous smirk wrapped around the cookie in his mouth. "His last name isn't Roche. But you called him Grandpa when you told the lady who taught you how to quodesh."

XAVIER BEGRUDGINGLY THREW the cookie bag onto the middle console after lots of begging and pleading. A rich cinnamon, chocolate, and sea salt scent rose from the gallon Ziplock, which Marge had filled to the brim with cookies.

The cookie smell mixed with a faint hint of Nicole's sweat in my brain...a sharp distasteful connection.

But Hazel and Ava and I all stuck our hands in the Ziplock bag straight away. I took one bite and had to lock my eyes on the road to keep from closing them in delight.

At this section of road, the trees fell away from us on either side. Tall grasses reached for the sky.

The sky itself stood bright blue like a bird's egg, close enough to touch and strong enough to drink as it hemmed us in on all sides.

It sparked my soul and I reached for the sky in front of us with a cookie-filled hand. Crumbs dropped to the dashboard, and I pulled my hand back. I took another bite of cookie, but the panic hit me right then.

My stomach turned. Marge had said it was almost lunch time.

Suzannah was probably texting my dead phone right about now, wondering where we were. "We've missed it!" I cried. "Bridesmaids were supposed to be there at eleven."

"Lauren." Hazel was beyond exasperated. "It's only seven forty-eight Pacific Daylight Time. Pay attention."

"But she said—" I started.

Hazel shifted away from me in her seat. Her shoulders were stiff like boards.

I took a deep breath. "I'm sorry. I didn't mean to..." As my words trailed off like unfinished roads, I realized that Hazel had been the one to tell me not to take Nicole on board. *If I had just listened to her, we wouldn't be in this mess. No wonder she's mad.*

"I trust you," I said. "Tell me what to do and I'll do it."

Hazel stared at her hands, which were folded on top of the ruffles of her red skirt. "We need to quodesh faster."

"What do you mean?"

She raised her head, looking straight ahead. "Finding Nicole and getting the ring back could take forever. We might not have time to drive to exit ten."

I glanced at my cookie in sudden disgust.

Setting it in the gray cup holder, where it nestled into the circular opening, I put both hands on the steering wheel and settled in to think. "So how—"

"Marge's websites."

I cocked my head.

"She said that they taught her to quodesh. Maybe there's secrets for doing it faster."

"But we don't have any working phones."

Hazel adjusted the wide strap of her white tank top. "Don't we?"

I glanced in the rearview mirror.

Hazel turned to me, her lips pressed together. She inhaled like an accordion wheezing. "We *need* to find a shorter way back. Otherwise there's no way we'll make it."

I kept my eyes on the road and lifted my chin to talk to the backseat. "Xavier, you can plug in your phone now. We need it to figure out our route."

Xavier spat out a response. "You're making a request, right?"

"Yes, I am." My tone grew hotter, boiling like steam in the car, the humidity hitting my face with a sudden slap. "Will you do it without arguing for once?"

Xavier sat upright. "You're not the victim here. *I'm* the one who got called a 'dirtbag' when I'm innocent."

Hazel slapped the charging cord into his hand. "Here."

He stretched it to the backseat, stuck the end into his phone, and retreated into brooding silence again.

We hit Indianapolis just like Marge said, and Hazel directed me back to Nicole's house. We parked underneath the same tree as we had the night before.

My heart beat-beat-beat in my chest as Hazel and I climbed out.

When Xavier's car door slammed, Hazel and I made eye contact. *Oh boy, here we go.*

I hurried to the front door before he could rush over and bang it down. I rang the doorbell and a twentysomething-year-old woman with *bright* yellow hair answered.

She looked only a few years older than my sister and I noticed the sunlight spark off a ring on her left finger.

The sun shone high overhead and my stomach growled.

Her smile faded to confusion. "Hello, how can I help you?"

I steeled myself. "Yes, we're looking for Nicole. We dropped her off here yesterday, and she has something that belongs to us. We're just here to get it back."

"Um..." The woman glanced behind her, where I could see a dark-stained wood staircase and a hallway leading to a glass sliding door. "I'm Brandy, her sister, but Nicole's not here."

Xavier stomped onto the porch, his fists clenched. "Where is the dirtbag?"

Brandy looked up at him, startled, and her grip tightened on the door handle. "I'm sorry, I don't know." And she shut the door.

The wreath swung on its nail and banged against the glass door with a *tap, tap, tap*. I moaned. "Where do we go now?"

"She's at a pawn shop." Xavier's voice was hard like bedrock.

I didn't have time for this. I just needed the ring back.

Even if my phone had stayed alive after the jump, I don't know if I could've handled telling Grandpa Mack that the ring had been stolen.

Stolen by the hitchhiker I had decided to pick up off the side of the road when I was in charge.

"Hazel, where's the nearest pawn shop?" I moved for the stairs, but Xavier blocked my path.

"You're too soft on her," he said. "She stole your sister's ring."

My heart beat-beat-beat in my chest. "Look, it doesn't matter. What's done is done. We just need to fix it."

Xavier stared down at me, his face twitching. The lines across his forehead sharpened as they creased even deeper. I could feel the anger pouring from him like smoke from a broken-down engine.

Maybe I should just leave him here and let Brandy take him in, since it looks like Nicole may or may not be coming back.

Maybe he'd shut up if I told him all about how I'd become a poor little orphan girl.

After that, maybe he'd even volunteer to leave my sister's wedding well enough alone.

I shoved his shoulder and he fell back onto the next step. "We're going to search the pawn shops and that's final. Will you please get out of my way?"

He stared at the spot on his chest where I'd pushed him. "That's how you need to treat Nicole, not me." He raised twitching hands and brushed off his shirt.

I clenched my fists. "I need you to cooperate for just five minutes and let me find my sister's ring and get to San Diego in time for the wedding." Frustration bled all over my voice. I shouldn't have pushed him, I just...I was trying to stay in charge. I was trying to be a leader.

And I had trusted my instincts. I bit my lip, a cold feeling washing over me like the rain last night.

I shivered even though humidity stuck to us like moths to lights. The bright green grass in the yard beyond Xavier appeared fake in the sunlight. He turned his sullen self around and started walking towards the car.

I crossed my arms over my stomach and followed. Faint freckles on my arms showed under the bright, sticky sun.

What now? Would we just drive from pawn shop to pawn shop, looking for Nicole? Or for the ring? Because she might've already sold it.

What would we do if she had? If we called the police to report it stolen, there was no way they'd let us leave with it in enough time to get to Suzannah's wedding. And there was no way to convince them we had a wedding to attend in San Diego anyways, because they didn't believe in quodeshing and the California wildfires blocked the way and we couldn't drive from Indianapolis to San Diego in a day.

I couldn't expect the police department to take that big of a leap of faith.

But could I buy back the ring? It had been expensive the first time and I had no clue how pawn shop pricing worked. Could we bargain for it? We only had two broken phones...and Xavier's ring. Which he probably wouldn't be needing now, but I didn't expect him to be giving it up anytime soon.

"Lauren?" The word poked me like a stick. I stopped in my tracks, about six feet away from the passenger side door of the car.

Hazel came up next to me. "Unless there's charge on Xavier's phone, I don't know how to get us to a pawn shop." She winced, her teeth pressed together.

I hunched my shoulders in tighter around myself, the way Nicole had yesterday in the backseat. Now I finally understood why she'd refused to eat any Starbursts. She'd felt guilty about stealing the ring. It made me sick.

To think she had been planning to do this the whole time. "God shouldn't give humans that power," she had said.

Why didn't I see it? Did Xavier see her do it? Did he know? I glanced at the floppy hair on the back of his head, his drooping shoulders, the way his feet stabbed at the sidewalk as he ambled towards the Highlander.

No way he knew, he would've told on her. And he'd had his own secrets to keep.

Was it a good thing he and Ava had broken up? That thought shocked me enough that I realized I'd zoned out, staring at the glimmers set into the sidewalk.

I shivered again. I had no clue if it was a good thing or not—I'd never been in a relationship before.

I felt the edge of words slipping in and out of my brain, something from the Holy Spirit maybe. *Ask me,* or something like that. I gripped my side tighter.

Was that God or was that something else? Why on earth would I ask for discernment about Ava and Xavier's relationship?

I didn't think either of them would listen to me if I *did* hear from God, and I really didn't want to. How could I trust I had heard right? They should really talk to Grandpa Mack about their problems. Maybe he could help them if they wanted to stay together.

Hazel brushed past me, catching the sleeve of my baby blue t-shirt with her shoulder. "You okay?"

"Uh, yeah," I said.

"I'll drive."

I stared at her for a second, her piercing green eyes forcing me to unravel the meaning of her words through the fog of my thoughts. "Okay. Thank you." I attempted to smile.

She held up her pair of keys in one hand, the plastic pieces clacking against each other. Her eyes searched mine.

Hazel walked around to the driver's side and I sat in the passenger seat. It felt like a lifetime ago when I'd planned on curling up in the passenger seat of the RV and catching up on assignments the whole way to California.

Right then, it felt like college might never come, that I might be stuck in this car for the rest of my life.

I was sick of this Highlander. I wanted the journey to be over.

"There's charge!" Hazel held up Xavier's phone triumphantly from the driver's seat.

“My phone is finally alive again, after an incredibly long time,” Ava exclaimed a moment later. A hand burst through the space between the front seats with a lit-up phone screen. It showed a battery with a low red dial and a charging plug moving up and down on the screen. “My turn to plug it in, at long last.”

“Um...” Hazel showed the screen of Xavier’s phone. “Only twelve percent.”

Awkward silence settled onto the backseat with a certain tension rising underneath.

“Can’t we stop and get another adapter?” Ava asked.

“No time,” Hazel said. “We only have a few hours. We might need to search every pawn shop in this city.”

I nodded, my arms tightening around my waist. The car sank into silence.

There was probably no way this would work, but I’d promised my sister I’d be there. How could I miss her wedding? I needed to bring the ring. Grandpa Mack had entrusted it to me.

And I had messed up.

Hazel got Xavier to enter his password and started the car on a path to the nearest pawn shop.

As we pulled onto a main road, I broke the silence. “If we don’t make it, Grandpa Mack doesn’t have his suit.” The words tasted bitter on my tongue. “He’s walking her down the aisle and handing her off to Dennis with nothing but khakis and a mothball-y old work shirt.”

“Or your dress,” Hazel said with a chuckle.

It didn’t hit me as funny. I stared at the road ahead.

“Sorry.” Hazel bit her lip.

“Don’t worry about it,” I answered. But my tone betrayed me. I wanted to sew my lips shut.

I turned my face to the window, watching the people passing over the paved walking trails. The hills rose and fell like waves.

I realized that Grandpa Mack and Suzannah didn't know where we were or why. Every passing second ticked closer to the ceremony.

I pulled my phone from the center console. The console had two normal-sized cup holders, the front one with my partly eaten cookie in the bottom and the second one with Xavier's phone upright and displaying maps like the glowing key to finding a new world.

I left the cookie to crumble in the cup holder and pressed the power button on my phone. Nothing. It was still dead.

GRANDPA MACK ALWAYS SAID LUCK was for people who didn't believe in God.

We drove around Indianapolis for two hours, bouncing from pawn shop to pawn shop like roadkill bounced around by cars.

I held my breath every time a cashier brought out a ring case. My stomach clenched every time I flipped it open to look inside. "What bad luck," Ava moaned every time it wasn't Suzannah's ring.

On our way to the thousandth place, we spotted Nicole.

She strode along the sidewalk, staring at the pavement, shoulders hunched, with her fingers cupped around something. I screamed and pointed.

She didn't notice us pull into a parking spot.

My heartbeat quickened. This was it. This was the time to get the ring back and—and—and somehow right all the wrongs.

We jumped from the car and piled onto the sidewalk behind Nicole. She didn't notice. She continued walking past a burnt brick building with foreclosure signs in the windows.

She strode along ten feet ahead of us, but within calling distance.

I didn't know what to say—was this a confrontation or should I stay kind and gentle? I didn't trust myself to pull off either.

"Hey, you!" Xavier stepped ahead of me, clenched his fists, and squared his feet.

I clenched my teeth, jolting to a stop before I bumped into him.

Nicole jumped and glanced to the side. But she kept going, like a wound-up music box.

Xavier shouted obscenities at a fever pitch.

Nicole stopped and turned, her feet pedaling underneath her in small steps, her body rotating like a spinning rack from one of those pawn shops. Her eyes shot wide in recognition, and she hid one hand behind her back.

"We know you have it," Xavier bellowed.

Ava stood on the other side of him, the half-burnt building behind her. Hazel stood to my right, her mouth twisted in thought. It felt like we'd all been frozen for the last thirty seconds except for Xavier.

I should do something. This was my battle. I took a step forward and held out my hand for the ring. "Just give it back, and we won't report you to the police or anything."

Nicole's face twisted, like she was a toddler deciding whether to throw a tantrum or not. I didn't feel old enough to be doing this—to try and act like I had some sort of authority. I had no clue what I was doing.

Ava's mouth dropped open. "Wait, you're literally offering her the chance to go off scot-free?"

"No time! I needed to get to my sister's wedding three hours ago." I took another step towards Nicole, my arm still outstretched.

No one else moved.

Nicole wore the same mom jeans and wrinkled gray shirt that she had yesterday.

I took another step, my hand insistently outstretched.

Nicole backed up, holding the ring to her chest. "N-no, I need it!" Nicole shouted. And she took off running in the other direction.

Ava squealed. Hazel grabbed my arm.

"She's got a five-second head start!" Xavier yelled.

We all pounded down the sidewalk after Nicole and my precious ring.

Xavier's footsteps soon thundered down the sidewalk ahead of me, his black sneakers like flags in the wind.

I ran four or five steps behind him, my heartbeat bouncing around in my ears faster than the rhythm of my footsteps.

Energy jolted through me and I started gaining ground.

I darted between a lamppost and the cars parallel parked on the street.

A fire hydrant appeared in front of me. I twisted and threw my arms out, but still banged my shin into the metal edge. "Ah!" I cried.

I lowered my head and continued sprinting. *This is for Suze!*

Nicole reached the intersection.

The main road, the one we had been driving on when we found her, was busy. But the crossroad was smaller and narrower.

Nicole ran past the pole with the crosswalk button. With only a half glance in each direction, she ran across the smaller road.

I veered to avoid the pole, almost ramming into the side mirrors of a black car parked there. Xavier grunted as he sprinted past me out onto the street, and I followed.

Nicole had reached the other side and stopped to pant, looking back at us.

Her eyes widened when she saw Xavier and I bearing down on her.

She jogged past a red brick restaurant and ducked into the open mouth of an alleyway.

"Come on, come on, come on," I cried as I caught up with Xavier.

I jumped onto the sidewalk and beelined for the alley.

My heart pounded and my focus narrowed until the dark opening filled my vision. *I can't let her get away.*

I swung around the corner and into the alley.

The darkness blinded me.

My own quick, light panting echoed as I blinked.

When Xavier's footsteps stopped, I heard the scratching, scrambling noise coming from the end of the alleyway.

My eyes started to adjust, and I could make out the shapes enough to creep forward.

Two dumpsters and a metal door lined the wall to our left. A fire escape dangled seven feet overhead to our right—the access point for a spiderweb of rusted metal cages stretching along the side of the building.

"Look around," Xavier growled. "There's no escape, right?"

The scratching noise grew more frantic.

I swallowed. "We can do this the easy way, or the hard way, but either way you're giving us back the ring." My raised voice echoed against the walls on either side. It sounded uncertain...like I was fourteen again.

I finally made out Nicole's form at the very end of the alley. She stood on an old crate, trying to climb a brick wall with her bare hands. She craned her neck, staring upward like the top of the wall was her exit number ten.

Her back was to us, her gray t-shirt sticking to her skin.

She threw a glance over her shoulder every few seconds, scrambling for a grip as I crept closer.

I hesitated when I reached the dumpsters. I glanced behind me and saw that Hazel and Ava had bottlenecked the narrow passageway.

When I looked back at Nicole, she was partway up the wall.

I sprinted towards her. Xavier shouted, joining me.

"Oof." Nicole lost her grip and fell a few feet.

The crate cracked and collapsed under her as she landed.

Nicole turned to face us, her back to the wall, her hands trembling. Her eyes focused on the fire escape overhead.

She ran and launched herself at it, left hand outstretched and right hand tucked to her side, holding the ring case. Her legs swung and her right tennis shoe hit Xavier in the stomach as he stood only two feet away from the fire escape hatch.

He doubled over with a grunt.

Nicole's fingertips smacked the metal bar with a reverberating twang, but she couldn't get a grip and so she fell. She landed on her feet, tottered, and faced us.

Her face was like a rubber ball, shifting from emotion to emotion with the elasticity of a children's toy. She looked down at the ring case clenched in her fist. "Is this y'all's?" she cried. "Is this y'all's?"

"Just give it back," I offered again. I kept my hands clasped in front of me, almost begging. Xavier crouched on the ground in front of her and I stepped closer, feeling like I should stand in front of him, but not brave enough to do it. "Give it back and everything will be okay. We won't report you to the police."

"It's the only way I can survive." Nicole's lip quivered.

"Your sister took you in though," I tried reasoning, "you're safe now. You're living with good people."

Nicole's face turned hard and dark hatred filled her eyes. "Bless your heart. People—people"—she tripped over her words, like she needed to spit out the bad taste of them—"have too much power. They always misuse it." Her gaze spread across the group and she pointed a finger straight at my chest. "That girl, y'all can't trust her. She'll ruin everything, and God didn't mean to give her power."

She looked at the ring case gripped in her right hand with a cool indifference. "That's why I'll be keeping this."

Xavier vaulted from the ground and grabbed for the ring.

She raised it into the air. She was taller than him, I realized as he jumped for it. When he grabbed both of her arms and jerked them down, she relented with a grunt.

He grabbed her fingers and tried to pry them open as she kicked his shins.

Nicole's other arm flailed as she tried to run away, but Xavier still held the hand with the ring case in it. "Assault!" she screamed. "Assault!"

Her words echoed down the narrow alley.

Xavier pried open her pointer and middle fingers, revealing the black velvet case.

I stepped forward, hands outstretched.

Nicole's free arm flailed as she tried to run, like she was underwater.

Her nails caught my face, sliding across my right cheek.

Her eyes, dark like grime-covered pennies, flicked to the corners of her eyes to see what she'd hit. They landed on me and her pupils narrowed to slits.

I lifted my hand to my cheek. Blood dripped from the scratch. I jerked to a stop, backed away from the struggling pair.

Xavier yanked the ring from under Nicole's thumb and turned his back to her. He cracked open the case and double-checked the ring was still inside.

Nicole dashed to the end of the alleyway.

I followed. “You’ll be okay,” I said to the back of her shirt. She leaned over like she was about to hurl her breakfast. “Just go to your sister’s house. She seemed nice.”

Nicole grabbed a board from the broken crate and whacked it against the sidewalk. Splinters flew and I took a step back, a small whimper escaping me.

She pivoted and raised the board above her head. Her eyes locked on me.

My heart beat-beat-beat in my chest. I covered my face.

Through my fingers, I saw Xavier dash behind her and wrap his arm around her neck.

Before I’d even finished scrambling backwards, Nicole slipped to the ground, her eyelids fluttering.

Her arms hung limp at her sides. Xavier propped up her torso, but her legs sprawled across the sidewalk. Her head swung like a rag doll’s, her chin coming to rest on her chest.

Xavier lowered her the rest of the way to the ground and took a step back. “Ta-da!” he crowed.

I stared at Nicole’s prone body.

Ava’s voice rose like a shrill siren. “What on this earth, Xavier Alex Smith?! If you strangled her, I’ll—”

“Relax,” Xavier said. “It’s a sleeper hold, babe. I saw it on TV.”

Hazel’s hands trembled as she knelt beside Nicole and put her ear to her chest. Her eyes widened as she listened.

I took one step closer to Nicole’s body, but rocked back, my eyes fixed on the limp muscles of her face. I flushed as red as the lipstick I used to draw on walls with.

With surgical precision, Hazel put two fingers on Nicole’s neck. After a deep breath, she spoke in a hushed voice. “She’s alive.”

Ava giggled like a laugh track, high and loud.

Xavier raised a bulging fist to the sky, the ring case trapped inside. "Run!" he yelled.

Without another word everyone sprinted from the alley and Nicole's still form. Hazel stayed, petrified, for a moment longer.

I looked back as I ran, and Hazel made eye contact. Her eyes begged me to say something. To take leadership.

My mouth worked as if I had a wad of gum inside. *I can't...he stole...* I didn't know what to do. So I ran.

The bruise on my shin ached as each of my steps punched a hole in the sidewalk.

We sprinted across the road and piled into the van. I ended up in the driver's seat with the key in the ignition and my hands on the wheel. Hazel got in last.

I peeled away from our parking spot, nervous laughter pouring from my mouth.

WE DROVE MILE AFTER MILE in silence. Adrenaline had pumped when we sliced through Indianapolis traffic, but now on the highway, all I could hear was road noise and all I could see was each exit number ticking down. 150...149...148...

I lifted my chin and examined my right cheek in the mirror.

Two jagged gashes cut across my face. One was longer, reaching from the bridge of my nose to my ear. Fingernail-sized streaks of blood had fallen from the deepest parts of each scrape and dried on my cheek.

I winced and fell back into my seat.

Exit number 147...

Snails could count faster than those miles worked themselves down. Grass could grow faster than those miles ticked down. Tomorrow could come faster than those miles whittled closer to the number we needed—exit number ten.

Hazel turned from the barren fields out the window and fiddled with her open notebook. "We left her there."

The car engine humming was her only response. Sun emanated through the windshield like a huge magnifying glass trying to set fire to our faces. I sagged in my seat.

"Lauren promised Nicole that she wouldn't call the police," Ava finally piped up.

"*If* she cooperated." Hazel closed her notebook. "She didn't."

No one commented on that.

Hazel pointed at the clock on the dashboard and continued. "Lauren's sister gets married in one hour and thirty-six minutes. We veered so far east that we're barely out of Indianapolis. There's no way we'll get there in time. We should turn around."

Ava's voice came out high-pitched. "She's next to a restaurant, so someone will find her sooner or later."

I had left Nicole unconscious in an alley. An alley. *Did she even know where she was and how to get back to her family's home? Would her family even take her in again?* She couldn't exactly explain why a bunch of nice kids had beat her up without admitting that she'd stolen an expensive ring.

Would they turn her into the police?

I couldn't exactly feel sorry, because she'd decided to do the wrong thing. She had used her power to do something evil, and she knew it.

"Guys?" Hazel's voice felt like someone pouring ice water over my head. She hunched over my phone. "Sleeper holds are a form of strangling. They can cause brain damage."

Inertia pushed me back into my seat. I felt like I was in a fighter plane and I looked at the gas dial. We had half a tank and were going 92 mph. I'd sped up without realizing it.

My heart pounded in my chest and whacked the bruise on my leg with each rush of blood. I hit the brake pedal hard, and we lurched to a slower speed.

I blinked tears from my eyes. Hazel's words were like a snowball rolling down a hill, gaining more and more momentum as it bounded across the slope.

Exit number 140.

I jerked onto the off-ramp without checking my blind spot and turned on the blinker in the direction of the nearest gas station. "I need to use the restroom," I said robotically.

I felt a shaking sensation in my gut, earthquake vibrations spreading from my core. I clenched my hands on the wheel so they wouldn't shake. My knuckles turned white. I checked both directions before turning onto the street from the off-ramp, feeling as if I only half saw what was in front of my eyes.

There weren't cars coming, right? There weren't cars coming.

Hand over hand I turned, jerking halfway through the arc as I realized I was veering into the lane of opposing traffic. I righted the curve and pulled us into the right lane. The gas station was only one light away.

The light was green. It was green, wasn't it? I actually wasn't certain if I ran a light or not, because I couldn't see it as green in my head—all I remembered was staring at the road. I parked in the gas station parking lot. The rush of blood filled my ears.

I turned the key, removed it, stuck it in my pocket, and went inside before anyone else had opened their car doors.

I crossed the parking lot, feeling as if I wouldn't see a moving car unless it hit me. I grabbed the hot black metal door handle and walked inside a KFC attached to the gas station. The smell of fried chicken turned my stomach.

The bathrooms were to the right of the KFC counter, in a little hallway between KFC and the gas station convenience store.

I walked the narrow, dim hallway and found the girl's bathroom.

I shut myself inside.

I paced the length of the graying linoleum floor. It was about ten feet wide, and my pacing avoided the dingy white toilet and sink along the left wall. I paced a square—along the wall with the door in it, then the empty wall, then the far wall until I was within a few feet of the toilet. "What's true? What's true? What's true? What's true?" I muttered to myself as I paced. *God, please help me.*

Suzannah's wedding is in an hour and a half.

I gripped the sides of the white porcelain sink. My thumbs thrust towards the drain, my other fingers gripping the undersides, and I leaned forward, bowing to the weight of the truth. *Nicole could be dying.*

Cold sweat raced down my forehead. *I failed as a leader, big time.*

I bit my lip as the last fact pounded like a nail in a coffin. *I can't make it to my sister's wedding. I tried my best...but I'm going to break my promise.*

I closed my eyes in a grimace and went back to muttering. "What is true? What is true? What is true?"

The truth is, God is good. And I can trust myself when I trust him.

My head shot upright at the lightning striking thought. "I—I—I *can*. That is true." I sucked in a breath, deep gulps of the sticky-sweet soap smell. "God is good. And I can trust myself when I trust him."

I pushed a looooong breath out like a sigh. Oxygen hit my brain like water from a squirt gun, and I started to be able to think again.

"Lord, is she dying?" I asked the question out loud. My voice echoed against the floor and ceiling tiles, cracking on the last word.

No. The word glowed like a neon sign in my brain.

I collapsed onto the toilet seat. *Thank God.*

After a moment, I stuck out my leg and wrinkled my nose at the bruise that had already formed where I'd run into the fire hydrant.

I wondered if Suzannah would want me to cover it with makeup for the wedding pictures? We could still take wedding pictures tonight, after we got there and before they left for the honeymoon.

I traced my finger along the bruise. The fire hydrant had hit me halfway up my shin. A bruise—bluish with dark purple blood spots and a yellow lump shaped like a jellybean in the middle—swelled in the impact zone.

"Nicole is unconscious in Indianapolis," I said out loud. I took another deep breath, pausing as my brain worked out its tangles. "Even though I probably won't make it to my sister's wedding ceremony now, I still want to get there as soon as possible. There's Grandpa Mack's suit..."

I trailed off, sorrow washing over me that he had to hand over his first granddaughter like this. I steadied myself and started again. "I don't have a phone number for Nicole's family. I don't know *anyone* else in Indianapolis...but *Grandpa Mack does.*" I grinned and the scratch on my cheek struck with pain. He'd told me that after we got the motel rooms last night!

Someone pounded on the door.

I jumped and started to limp towards it.

I glanced around to make sure I wasn't leaving anything in the bathroom and realized I should clean the cut on my face.

I mad-dash splashed water and soap on it, noticing the ragged-edge scrape on my arm when I looked in the mirror.

It was from the tree back at that gas station, from yesterday, and it hadn't closed up yet. I grabbed a brown paper towel and held it to my dripping clean cheek. It stung.

I opened the door, blushed at the girl in her late twenties holding a little boy by the hand. He looked just like her—obviously her kid. I slipped into the hallway.

The smell hit me like a semi. My mouth watered, my knees buckling as my brain turned to mush.

That Kentucky Fried Chicken smelled heavenly.

I'd left my purse in the car. Without the ring inside, I hadn't needed to take such good care of it anymore—although I guess I hadn't taken such good care of it in the first place. I pushed that thought aside. I needed my wallet to buy some lunch.

My stomach leapt at the thought. I hadn't eaten anything in hours except a few bites of cookie.

I slipped through the gas station stands. Hot dogs roasted over black slabs, radiating heat like an asphalt road radiated a mirage.

I unlocked Hazel's Highlander and crawled inside the driver's seat. No one was there, but they'd left Xavier's phone plugged into the cigarette lighter adapter.

I grabbed my bag and his phone. Hazel had convinced him to temporarily turn off the password until we all had working phones again. "To prove I'm not a criminal," he had grumbled as he did it.

This was perfect! I could call Grandpa Mack now. I dialed his number and my eyes fell on the cookie in the console as it rang.

"Well now," Grandpa Mack answered with his normal unshakeable stamina. "What's yer problem, Xavier?"

"Grandpa Mack," I said around a mouthful of cookie. Water continued to drip from my cheek, and I pressed the brown paper towel harder against my wound.

"Sweetheart," he said. Grandpa Mack always told me that my smile was like the sun. Now his smile lit up his voice and wrapped around me. "How's yer journey?"

I drank in the comfort of his voice as I swallowed the cookie. "I have a really long story for you, but basically we picked up a hitchhiker yesterday and right now she's in an alley in Indianapolis, unconscious, and no one knows where she is except us."

"Well now..." I could hear in his voice that he knew I wasn't done talking yet.

"Can you pray for her?" My voice cracked.

"Yes, ma'am." Grandpa Mack fell silent for a moment, and I knew he was praying in his head.

I took a deep breath. "She needs help. But we're an hour away so I was wondering if you could call your friends in Indianapolis and ask if they could go take care of her. We can't call the police...well at least, I don't know what will happen if we call the police."

"Could ya describe 'er location, sweetheart?"

"Yes, she's in an alley next to a brick apartment building at the corner of Pine Street and some boulevard. There's a restaurant next to her, but I don't know the name of it." My brain cells danced with adrenaline as I told him this. He'd ask how she'd gotten there next... and I would have to tell him.

A pen scratched on his side. "Do ya know 'er name?"

"Nicole," I said breathlessly. My heart was beating in my throat. Sweat dripped down my sides, mostly from the heat of the car. I slipped the strap of my purse onto my right shoulder and pulled the door handle. The car door cracked open, but I paused.

What was the charge at? Should I take Xavier's phone charger? I didn't have the wall outlet block thingy...

Leave it. A voice gently entered my thoughts, sounding the same as the voice I'd heard in the bathroom. Was that...God?

I stared through the windshield at the glazed parking lot, unseeing.

I snapped back into focus, realizing I should ask him to give Suzannah a message. "How's the wedding preparation going? How's Suze?"

"I pray 'er heart calms iffen it can." Grandpa Mack sighed lightly. "Dennis ain't been able ta help, either. He's chomping at the bit."

I nodded. "Now that Nicole will be okay, we'll drive without stopping until we get to San Diego." *Again,* I added in my head.

"Well now. Care ta tell me why Nicole's unconscious in an alley?" Grandpa Mack finally asked.

My stomach growled and I shoved the car door open the rest of the way. "I left her there after we fought with her over the ring. Oh—she stole Suzannah's ring. That's why we fought with her. She was about to hit me with a broken board," I took a deep breath, "and Xavier did a sleeper hold on her." My heart palpitated. *She's been there an hour already.* I wished I'd called Grandpa Mack earlier.

Grandpa Mack paused. "Iffen thet's the case, I'll hurry and call my friends in Indianapolis. They'll care fer 'er." More scratching sounds on his end. "I'm proud of ya." He said it like he was slathering thick pink frosting on a happy birthday cake.

We hung up and I walked into the KFC. It smelled like mac and cheese and mashed potatoes slathered in butter. Mmmm.

I just needed to grab food and drive as fast as safely possible. I didn't have the heart to tell him we might not make it, especially with Suzannah freaking out. Maybe we could get there in time for the reception. We'd see.

Hazel ran from a booth as soon as I entered the restaurant. "I found it!"

"What?"

"We can make it!"

My mouth dropped open and saliva dripped onto my chin.

Hazel didn't notice.

I wiped saliva from my face. "In time for the wedding?"

She nodded. "Come."

I followed her along the line of booths. She and Ava had bought me chicken strips and a tub of mashed potatoes. I dug into the mashed potatoes while Hazel explained.

Xavier and Ava sat across from each other on the inner side of the booth, holding hands across the table, their elbows propped on the table and both hands clasped as they looked into each other's eyes.

I'd had better company in the bathroom than Hazel in the restaurant from the looks of it.

"It's the quodeshing website." Hazel waved her arms like she was conducting a symphony. "Some people quodesh without an exit. God takes them where they need to go!"

I shook my head. "What do you mean without an exit?"

"Guardrails." Hazel said the word with a sort of reverence.

"Huh?"

Hazel sighed. "They just drive into the guardrails and God takes care of the rest. We gotta try it."

"Hold up. You want me to drive off the road in your brand-new car? Are you seriously okay with this?"

Hazel tilted her head at me. "Of course. We won't do it unless God tells you it's okay."

AS HAZEL BOUGHT another blue Gatorade and Ava disappeared to who knows where, Xavier returned from the restroom and sat at the booth across from me.

His leg jittered underneath the table.

I took my last bite of mashed potatoes and made eye contact. This should be good. Was he gonna beg me not to consider Hazel's death-wish plan or demand an apology for accusing him of stealing the ring? It was worth noting that his girlfriend was the one to do that, but you know, I was willing to apologize. "I'm sorry this ruined your proposal—"

He cut me off with a bewildered look. "I came to give you this." He brought his arms above the table and set the black velvet ring case down in the middle of the beige speckled table.

I stared at it.

Xavier hid his hands under the table again. "I don't care if I miss the wedding, but I care if you do, and I care if your sister doesn't have this."

I lowered my plastic fork into the cookie-cutter-shaped container the mashed potatoes had come in. The container still held spots of gooey mashed potato on the sides in stark contrast to the immaculate ring case.

"It's...hard..." Xavier stared at the table, head down, jaw working, "to move forward when you don't know"—his voice cracked—"if your parents will show up."

I blinked at him and I was sure sympathy crossed my face.

Instead of accepting it, he jerked his head at the ring case.

I reached for it, the velvet soft against my palms as I closed both hands around it.

I flipped the lid up and it snapped open to reveal the ring. Still pristine, the kite-shaped diamond took my breath away. The sun from the window sparkled on the ring like a promise. *We can make it in time. We can make it in time.*

I studied the twining black vines, the curve of the ring, the three diamonds set like scoops of ice cream piled on top of one another.

I touched the black gold with my shivering pointer finger. It felt cold. Like the Colorado that Suzannah would honeymoon in and the Colorado where I would go to college and the Colorado where our parents had lived.

Some part of me knew I was going home.

I snapped the ring case closed. My back straightened, and I knew it was time to seek the Lord. Time to pray about whether we could quodesh without an exit or not. Time to ask if it was safe.

Xavier nodded at the ring case with an uneasy smile. "It's great she didn't sell it, right?"

"She'll be okay," I said without thinking. "I told some friends where she is and they're going to take care of her."

His eyes widened and then closed, and he gave me a sharp nod as he turned his face away.

I tucked the ring back into my purse. *My precious.*

The light fell from the window onto the top half of my purse, the bottom half shielded by the sill of the window and the brick of the building.

The geometric patterns looked nicer with the half light, half dark background.

I kept my eyes fixed on the purse and asked a simple question in my head. *Is it safe to quodesh without an exit? Will you get us there?*

The voice came back like an exhale, a cool spring breeze with the sound of babbling brook and the smell of fresh, blooming flowers. And it said one word: *Yes.*

If only I could believe it.

"OKAY," I SAID as we reached the highway on-ramp. Butterflies bounced around my stomach. "We're about to merge."

Hazel glanced at me from the passenger seat, where she had charge of my purse and the ring. She hugged it in her lap, along with the blue Gatorade bottle clasped in her hand. "Nervous?"

I laughed, high like a hyena. "Why would I be nervous? We're just gonna drive off the road." I took a deep breath. "Yep, just drive off the road."

Hazel gulped her Gatorade. Sun shone through the blue liquid in the bottle and splotched her face with blue light. "God said 'Okay.'"

"Yep. He did, he did, so it's okay." I gripped the steering wheel as cars zoomed past me. I couldn't seem to move faster than 40 mph, and cars were changing lanes to go around me as I merged. "I really don't even know why I'm talking—I think I'm just nervous and that's why I'm talking."

Ava shifted in the backseat. “Uhhh, we’re incredibly aware of your nerves, ‘fearless leader.’”

I shrugged, my neck muscles stiff.

“She’s never steered us wrong,” Xavier said, leaning back in the seat with his arms folded and propping his legs on the center console. “We’ll make it.”

I glanced at his chunky black shoes, aware of the trees passing us on the passenger side. Remembering driver’s ed class where they told us that if you hit something, everyone’s heads jerked in the direction they were going beforehand. So Hazel’s head would hit the window, I would fall on Xavier’s feet...

I grit my teeth. Not helpful.

“Xavier, what on earth...at the very least put your seatbelt on!” Ava scolded from the backseat.

I glanced in the mirror again. Sure enough, his seatbelt wasn’t strapped and his eyes were closed. “It’s a quick power nap,” Xavier said. His clean-shaven lips turned up at the corners. “We could use some beauty sleep before the wedding, right?”

“It would help me extremely if you did it with your seatbelt on,” Ava dictated.

I tapped the brakes. “I’m not going anywhere until you buckle up.”

Hazel glanced at me. “You’re going thirty-five.”

I glanced at the speedometer. Yep. I was. “Put on your seatbelt,” I said fiercely as I sped up. We hit 50 mph and I evened out, not wanting to speed up much more.

A click came from the backseat. “You happy?”

“Very,” Ava intoned.

“Here we go,” I said breathlessly.

I turned on the blinker.

Hazel grabbed the handle hanging from the ceiling by her window. It looked like a trolley handle and I hadn't noticed it before. Xavier's toes shifted. Ava gasped.

I turned on my hazards so the cars would keep going around me. If I had to slow down to 15 mph or something, I didn't need a rear-ender.

I focused on the edge of the highway to our right. It was a nice strip of trees in a break between guardrails. A little ditch stood between us and flat green grass that ran for ten or twenty feet before it hit the tree line. It was the perfect place.

What's the speed limit? I asked, already veering towards the shoulder.

Sixty-five, leaped out at me.

"Sixty-five!" I yelled, hitting the brakes unintentionally. "He says sixty-five. He says sixty-five!"

I was going forty.

In the space it would take me to speed up, we'd pass by the nice, flat even spot that I'd picked out and hit the very end of a new guardrail starting. We'd splice the car in half.

The Highlander sped up even more, hitting 42 mph now. I needed to gun it or back out. It was now or never!

We headed straight for the edge of the guardrail.

Hazel reached for the quodesh dial with shaky hands.

She flipped it.

I jerked the steering wheel back towards the road, inside the safe white lines, my breath coming in tight gasps. I needed another minute. I needed another minute.

Hazel swayed, her arm jerking in its socket as she still held the overhead handle.

"Oof," came from the backseat and Xavier's legs disappeared.

"Snickerdoodles," he said in the lowest, most ominous growl I have ever heard.

I would've laughed if my heart hadn't been pump-pump-pumping in my chest too hard to breathe.

Xavier poked his head through the seats. "I thought we were going?"

"I couldn't do it. It was way faster than I thought..." I pulled in air through my nose, the stink of skunk hitting me. Great, more roadkill. "We just need to wait for another break in the guardrails and we'll try again."

Xavier grunted. Hazel gave me an encouraging nod. I glanced at Ava in the backseat. She was tapping on her phone.

Xavier's phone was still plugged into the car, offering directions to the wedding venue. We had forty-five minutes to get there or break my promise.

The directions were useless until after I quodeshed us there.

Hazel waved a hand in front of her nose. *What if we're about to become roadkill?*

I crinkled my own nose and watched the guardrails to our right, speeding up to 65 mph. They kept going, each post ticking off in my head with a *da-dum, da-dum, da-dum* like they were speed bumps I was hitting.

It felt like we were looking for the right exit number again, but this time I didn't need to wait for anything.

I just wanted to wait for a place with no guardrails. But God had said yes, so...

"Alright." I sighed and let the adrenaline rise up in my body. I turned on the blinker and checked my blind spot. "Let's do this," I said with determination.

And I drove into the rails.

WHAT IF I HEARD WRONG? The thought ran through my head in the slo-mo split second between turning the wheel and hitting the rails. I could see each metal bolt holding the guardrails together in stark detail...each blade of grass sprouting around the cross-shaped metal biting into the dirt at the base of one rail...the trees in full leaf a few feet past that.

I can trust myself when I trust God.

Shimmers appeared around the quodesh dial, sparkling like a firework stick in front of Hazel's face. Her mouth had dropped open even as she gripped the dashboard of her car with white knuckles. Her eyes sparkled extra green in reflection.

I gripped the steering wheel firmer as I realized I'd need to steer on the other side of this.

The front bumper hit the guardrail silently. White metal crumpled and the hood wrenched open and hung in front of the windshield, but the Highlander didn't jerk or shake like it should've. It was just the mirage.

Everything floated for a moment, gravity releasing its hold.

I checked the speedometer and hit the acceleration. I'd hit the brakes when it looked like the front of the car had hit the rails and we'd dropped below 65 mph.

Ava screamed, a high-pitched, monster-under-my-bed scream. "You're a maniac! You're a maniac! I cannot believe I decided to get in a car driven by you even after everything that's happened...it's not my time to die." She sobbed in Xavier's arms.

Hazel and I crossed the quodesh line and everything cleared up. We could see the bumper, which was uncrumpled, and the hood, back in its rightful place.

Wonderful desert heat waves pounded on the undamaged white metal of the hood and bounced up to create the effect of looking over top of a griddle while hamburgers sizzled.

"Open your eyes," Xavier shouted in the backseat, trying to get Ava to hear him over her crying.

We were on an exit, one of those exits where you have to switch lanes and merge onto a new highway almost immediately.

"Get over," Hazel pointed at the left lane.

I checked my rearview mirror.

A zippy black car was in the left lane, right where I needed to be—jet black and low to the ground with side mirrors sticking out like ears.

I flipped on my left blinker.

No response.

I was running out of space to change lanes before I missed the on-ramp. I hit the gas. *Thanks God, for making me go sixty-five instead of fifteen.* The speedometer hit 70-something as I screeched across the white line.

I sped up even more to keep them from rear-ending me and merged onto the highway like I was making a getaway. My head buzzed with all I'd just done. "What time is it?"

Hazel powered Xavier's phone. "1:27 PM local time."

"My sister gets married in thirty minutes." I blinked at the road, my stomach pressing back into the seat behind me as I sped up even more. "How far away are we?"

We were on a broad Californian highway with five lanes, the farthest left lane reserved for carpooling and marked with HOV signs every couple hundred feet. Angry hornet black-and-yellow paint marked the lane as if to scare me off, but I wasn't anywhere near it.

I moved to the middle lane and passed a car. Three cars zoomed past in other lanes, like Lightning McQueen in a race. No mountains were in sight here—only the wide-open desert and palm trees sprouting around us like brides with bowed heads.

"Three minutes," Hazel said, her voice sounding like it had been dipped in honey. "God's so good."

I laughed. "Of course he is."

"Here," she nodded at exit number one.

It must've been something crazy to watch for the drivers back in Illinois—to see a car wheel out of control, crash, and then disappear into thin air before the clang of crumpled metal could sound.

I turned on my blinker and checked behind me.

The red car was still there, chasing me. But it didn't matter because I was about to get off.

I checked the quodesh dial, still set for CA, and crossed the line to the off-ramp.

I hit the brakes hard. We all felt the pull of gravity as we slowed to a stop.

Hazel grabbed her seatbelt. "Left."

A huge smile spread over my face. "We're gonna make it! We're gonna make it to the wedding!" I cheered and everyone joined me, whooping and hollering.

We pulled into the huge circular driveway of the wedding venue only two minutes later. The best man's parents had agreed to host it on their beachside property.

The house stood tall like beach grass and elegant as a wedding cake. It was white, two stories tall, and enormous.

I parked crooked at the end of the line of cars which filled the circular driveway. I recognized a catering van, my sister's car, Dennis's car, and the cat slinking into the catering van.

Suze had sent me pictures of that cat, because she adored cats, but it was supposed to be locked in the house for the wedding.

I took my stuff from Hazel, savoring the feeling of the ring case in my grip. It fit nicely into my hand, the black velvet smooth to the touch.

"Xavier, can you grab that cat?" I pointed at the gray tail sticking out from the open door of the catering van. "It's supposed to be in the house."

He sighed and propelled himself out of the car.

We all climbed from the Highlander like we hadn't seen dry land in years. I tried to stride confidently to the front steps of the house, but my legs hitched at the first steps.

They'd become so used to the cramped position of driving that I had to stretch them out before I could walk.

A large wooden signboard, painted white, stood next to a path leading around the house. The crisp black letters read: "Welcome to Dennis and Suzannah's Wedding! Please Follow This Path for Seating." Two bouquets of lilac and greenery draped tastefully from the sign.

I mounted the front steps. The house felt hushed from the outside.

Hazel and Ava trailed after me with armfuls of clothing bags and suitcases, rustling with each step.

I reached for the doorbell, aware of my plain blue shirt and athletic shorts. I listened to the chimes through the glass pane set into the door, rehearsing what I needed to say to the caterer or whoever wasn't so busy that they answered. *I'm the bride's sister, where should I go?*

If they didn't believe me, the ring case clasped in my hand should be proof enough.

Dennis opened the door.

His jaw dropped open and I could read both excitement and apprehension in his eyes.

I held out the ring, but he brought me into a hug. His shirt smelled like vanilla, amber, and cedar. I craned my neck backwards to look at him.

Dennis pulled away, his hands still gripping my shoulders on either side. "You made it safe, sound, *and* on time." He looked sharp in his black tux and white shirt, almost like a different person than the one I'd met before, except for his ears.

He had perfectly rounded ears, pink on the tops. I wondered if they were pinker from nervousness today. He buzzed a little with excitement, but mostly he was just as grounded as always. "All good?" he asked, surveying Ava and Hazel gathering behind me.

"Yes," I answered.

He released my arms and opened the door wider. "Come in, come in."

I stepped into the marble foyer as he opened the door. Broad white steps curved in front of me, marble and windows and white couches marking everything around us. I felt like I'd stepped into a fairytale castle.

Xavier lunged through the doorway then, holding the cat.

"You found it—good for you, and thank you," Dennis said.

I was surprised he called the cat "it" instead of her. He reached for the cat, but I inserted myself between them.

I cradled the ring case in both hands. "Here."

Dennis turned his head and I caught a glimpse of stray brown hairs on his chin. His mom and Suzannah hadn't reminded him to shave, I guess. Or he hadn't caught a glimpse of them in the mirror. I should warn him that Suzannah liked clean-shaven men.

Dennis extended a hand, the white cuffs of his shirt hugging his wrists.

I pressed the soft velvet case into his hand, closing his fingers over the expensive ring with my own.

I looked him in the eyes. He had blue-green, veiled eyes, like a pond without a single ripple in its surface.

He smiled and the little hairs on his chin tilted. "Thank you, Lauren. Our gratitude, and rejoicing, abounds."

I dropped my hands. "You missed a spot shaving."

He tucked the ring case inside the pocket of his suit coat. His expression turned sober. "Thanks, and Suzannah wants to see you," he said.

AS KIDS, MY SISTER was always tall enough to tuck me under her arms and rest her chin on my head whenever she held me in a hug. By the time I graduated high school, I'd grown enough that she had to tilt her chin up to do that.

She sat before the vanity like a princess. It was white, with a huge mirror and vines and flowers hanging down the sides—I recognized them as the same lilacs and ivy as on the sign outside. A small circular light sprouted from the table, its silver stand aimed at the mirror. The train of her dress draped over the wicker bench she sat on.

The dress was off the shoulder, and all I could see from here was the open back showing the faint impressions of her shoulder blades and lace flowers ruffling around her arms.

Grandpa Mack stooped behind her, a weathered hand resting gently on her bare shoulder.

I stopped dead in my tracks. "You look beautiful," I breathed.

She turned. “Lauren!” It sounded like a scolding. She wore heavy makeup overshadowing her amber eyes, and her pouting lips had been painted a rich, powdery red. “Tell me where you’ve *been* for the last twenty-four hours! Why haven’t you been answering my calls?”

“My phone died.” As I answered, I felt something deep down in me like the pull that water must feel when it’s forming an eddy.

“The cat ran loose so no one could catch her—”

“Well—” I started but she surged on.

“—The decorations blew away in the wind, the best man still wants music for *his* entrance, and there was nobody but Daphne and the wedding planner to deal with it! Not to mention—”

“Well now. Yer menfolk were helpful,” Grandpa Mack supplied his own addendum. “Not to mention his folks.” He wore an off-white button-up shirt today, tucked into his khakis and ironed.

“Well, I have good news.” I smiled. “We caught the cat and I gave Dennis the ring, and Ava has Grandpa Mack’s suit outside.”

Suzannah looked at the mirror. “It’s a shame...” she whispered to herself. She lifted her head to stare at Grandpa Mack in the mirror. “Change into your suit, please. You need to hand me off in something other than *that*.”

He slipped past me with a whispered, “Be gentle with her, sweetheart,” and a kiss on the forehead.

I stepped out of the doorway and into the room, taking a seat on the bed behind the vanity. It was a small bedroom. The owners probably had five guest bedrooms just like it.

The centerpiece of the room was the vanity, but a whole set of matching white furniture graced the rest of the room. The open closet door revealed empty hangers waiting for something, and one window shone bright warm light on the white bedspread.

Suzannah messed with the makeup cases on the vanity, shoulders tight. "I wanted you to be a bridesmaid."

My mouth dropped, my heart pounding. Had she really just said that? "Do you still?"

My heartbeat filled my ears as I waited for her answer.

Suzannah spun around on the stool. Her hair swooped from her forehead to rest in a mermaid braid on her right shoulder. The braid reached to her waist. Tiny white flowers had been woven into it, stems and all, at various points amid the curls and braiding.

I wanted to tell her that it looked amazing.

But she seemed to be considering kicking me out of her wedding, so I bit my tongue.

What could I say in a situation like this? I clenched the edge of the bedspread with my hands. My knuckles started to turn white.

Suzannah twisted her hands around each other, rubbing the spot on her finger where a ring had left a tiny tan line. She grabbed her engagement ring from the surface of the vanity and slipped it on her ring finger. Her words came out loud and soft at the same time, like water hits your face in the shower. "I needed you."

"I'm sorry." *It's not like I traveled across half the country to get here.* I waved a hand at her ensemble. "You didn't need me to look gorgeous."

"That's not what I meant." Her shoulders curved inward and she crossed one arm over her stomach, the other hovering over her chest. Her face darkened as she thought.

The scrape on my cheek pulsed and I huffed a breath. "Do you need 'proof' that I tried my hardest to get here? Because I can give you proof." I slammed a pointing finger onto my cheek, touching the end of the raw, curved red scrape. It stung.

Suzannah flicked her eyes upward. Eyeshadow loomed over her pupils like storm clouds over a mountain.

I revealed the inside of my forearm, pointing at the light red line that looked like a thread had been sewed into my arm.

Then I turned as if posing for a photo and waved a hand at my shin. The ugly bruise still had a sickly yellow lump at the center.

Suzannah stared at the carpeting.

I took a step closer, my head spin-spin-spinning. "Should I go cover these in makeup so they don't ruin your perfect wedding?

She sucked in a breath, the air whistling in the narrow space between her lips, and she blew it out again like spitting out vodka. "I can't do this."

My breath caught in my throat. This was the last thing I'd expected to happen when I got here. I blurted out the question even as I already knew the answer. "You can't do what?"

"Marry Dennis." Unshed tears magnified her eyes like a water glass set on top of two copper pennies. Her voice cracked—a hostage pleading her case before the desperado, lips bleeding and mouth unused to moving.

"But—but—don't you love Dennis?"

Suzannah lowered her perfect eyebrows. "It was stupid to try rushing the ceremony."

My words rolled around my mind like a gumball spinning down the track of a gumball machine. I had this sense that I didn't really know what we were talking about anymore. "You did it for his mom." My words faltered as they took their first steps into the world.

Suzannah straightened her shoulders. "She's not my problem."

My mouth fell open and an unintentional scoffing sound escaped. "She's about to be your mother-in-law."

Suzannah's eyes flashed with anger. She stood, one hand on her hip and the other clenching the air. The dress moved with her gracefully. Pure white, the neckline low enough to show a little something, lace-laden and flower-filled, merging into the shining fabric around her waist. The white fabric of the dress fell loosely to the floor, but over it lay a veil of gauze and lace extending in a two-foot train. She didn't look lanky in that dress.

Her words came out like lemon juice. "Who are you to say that I should marry him? It's not like you heard from God or anything."

I felt each word flash like a knife blade on my tongue. "Well, do you want me to ask him?"

Her mouth dropped open and her eyes widened. She crossed the room and grabbed my hands like a drowning woman grasping at a life preserver. "That's perfect! I need you to tell me what's true."

Oh no. I opened my mouth. "I—uh—I—um..."

"It's a shame you weren't here earlier. Lauren, I need this."

"I—why didn't you ask Grandpa Mack?"

Her hands pressed together as she dropped onto the bed next to me. "Lauren, don't you understand...?" Her lips curled upward around the words. "He's not my sister."

The tight fist around my heart unclenched, like the tide receding on its daily pilgrimage back towards the horizon.

"Oh—okay." I felt myself blushing. I paced from the bed to the vanity. "Give me a minute."

"The ceremony is fifteen minutes away."

Suzannah watched me hopefully from the bed as I paced. *God, should Suzannah marry Dennis? I...I think they should, but I don't know. You're God, so if you could tell me, that would be great.*

I cringed at my own words. Oh well, he would understand. *You've taught me that you're good, and I can trust you.* I was starting to get dizzy from pacing, so I stood still. *I'm listening.*

And I listened.

I listened to static. Like a car radio when you're driving in the middle of nowhere, I didn't pick up anything. Just the jittering, bouncing sound of static. I closed my eyes and heard my own inhale and exhale.

Static.

I stuck my hands in the pockets of my shorts, balling the internal fabric into fists.

Static. Stifling static, and then...peace.

I listened to my inhale and exhale again. I released the pocket lining in my fists and my hands sagged in relief. *It's okay,* scrawled across my brain in sparkling golden letters.

I sighed. *Thank you, God.*

I felt the need to kneel.

I lowered myself to the ground, shifting to avoid putting pressure on my bruised shin. Suzannah would get married in fifteen minutes...or not.

It all depended on this...on what I heard from God. And if I heard wrong?

I couldn't think about that. I knelt even lower, putting my arms and face to the ground in a bow before the king of the universe.

God, what do I need to say?

Nervousness pricked at my stomach. The carpet smelled of sheeny vacuum powder, the strands luxuriously fine against my forehead.

The darkness before my eyes swam as a warmth spread through my chest. *God, I trust you.* And at the edge of my brain, I felt words coming like oncoming traffic.

Every force of light in my brain focused in on that one spot, a diamond glittering in a case, and the words emerged. *Grow as you go.*

I peeled my face from the floor. Blood rushed to my head as I rose to my knees, certainty coursing through me. "I think I'm hearing...'grow as you go.'" The words gained power as they left my mouth and I almost heard the echo in my core. A pulsing of my heart with the words in that space of silence.

Suzannah's face convulsed and she pressed her left hand to her mouth, the engagement ring shining like a teardrop on her ring finger.

I took a deep breath.

She kept her eyes on mine, something welling deep inside them.

I hesitated. My bruised shin hurt from kneeling, so I pulled my legs under me to sit crisscross applesauce. I rubbed my shin, peeking at Suzannah.

Muffled cries came from underneath her palm, but she lifted her shining amber eyes to heaven. She blinked and they grew shinier, not releasing their bounty of emotion yet.

A question grew in my chest, rolling into a snowball. I felt in my gut that I needed to voice it. "Grow into what?" I finally asked.

"Commitment—" Suzannah choked on the wet word. "It's...I've been scared I won't have the strength." She blinked again and a big ol' tear escaped her eye. "Because what if he gets deathly ill and it's contagious...and I *run?*" The tear traced its way down her cheek, leaving two streaks of concentrated blush on either side of its path.

I swallowed hard.

"Suze..." My voice trembled and I gripped my hands together and tucked them under my chin. I pressed my chin against my hands, holding them to my chest.

The whole day hit me all at once—the whole trip...Xavier asking and asking about my parents, Ava agreeing with me about the whole tragic backstory thing, Nicole saying, "You poor girls..."

Grandpa Mack handing me the ring, sending me ahead so that I could make it to the wedding rehearsal because he didn't need practice walking a girl down the aisle.

His girl. He'd lost his girl.

My heart squeezed in my chest. Our mom.

Suzannah slid her hand down until it didn't cover her mouth anymore. She swiped tears from her eyes with the pads of her fingers. "Because what if she made the wrong choice?" Her face twisted in pain. "What if she'd chosen us instead?"

I...I couldn't think anymore. My own face crumpled with unshed tears.

Our parents had met at CCU. Neither of them had failed out, and after they graduated, they got married. They joined a mission organization and after a few years of training and Suzannah's birth, they shipped out to Papua New Guinea.

Once there, they had me. A little less than four years later, our papa caught a deadly disease. In the remote village they lived in, in nothing more than a wooden shack with a dirt floor, there was no doctor.

The radio had broken and a flight wasn't expected for another two weeks. The local tribal chief forbid anyone to trek across the jungle and find help for the white preacher man.

We had no medicine, no medical kit, and no chance of survival.

Our mom had committed to being by her husband's side until the very end. And she was. Until the very last breath.

Tears dripped down my cheeks as I mouthed my mom's maiden name: Isabella Stevens.

She had breathed her last a few days later according to our best guesses.

We didn't even know the exact date she'd died. We didn't know why she hadn't tried to escape to a city until a missionary later uncovered our mom's journal.

She'd written last on November 4th, 2003:

I have no hope of making it through the jungle to Tabubil with a four and seven year old in tow. I sent them both to live with Putri as soon as Daniel started to cough. I fear I've already caught the disease, so I beg for their lives. She will, with the chief's help, take care of them if we die. If only because my father will pay for their safe return. All I hope and pray is for our children to make it out alive. God is able to take them unscathed from here. I cry to think we won't see them grow up...my beautiful Suzannah who's such a little mom already and little Lauren with joy as bright as the sun.

Tear marks had marred the page. Suzannah had pored over the whole journal as a kid, and Grandpa Mack discussed it all with her while I played with Barbies on the carpet.

It never seemed to concern me much...God had a plan and I had Grandpa Mack. Who needed parents?

Of course, on hard days or big occasions I missed them. When I missed them, I replayed my memories.

I remembered happy bits and pieces of living in that little shack surrounded by the jungle before anyone got sick.

I remembered the sun sparking the red in my dad's hair when I peered up at him one time, how it had seemed like he was on fire. In the pictures his hair looked brown, but Suzannah and I knew it wasn't really.

I remembered crying and screaming while my mom tried to change my outfit; how she held my flailing arms with cold hands and guided them into the sleeves. I don't even know what I was upset about.

I remembered Suzannah telling me about when they got sick, and after that our memories jumbled together into a fruit punch.

The tribal chief had buried them with ceremony. I don't know why, but he decided to honor the white man preacher after he was dead.

Grandpa Mack flew to Papua to pick us up after days and days of the local women taking care of us. Suzannah had spent the time shooing them away from me, convinced that everyone had the plague now and couldn't be trusted to touch her sister.

Suzannah released a hicuppy sigh. "How could she commit to 'til death do us part'?"

I started to respond but found a big ol' lump in my throat like a piece of the mountains had lodged itself there. I swallowed. I felt the sky swirling in my chest, not feeling like a void, but a door—a shimmering quodesh opening, expanding my world from the inside. "God said you can grow as you go, didn't he?"

"But will God follow through on his word?" Suzannah grimaced, the whites of her teeth showing as creases marred her forehead and circled her nose. "He allowed our parents to die when they were serving him." The quality of her anger and desire touched something in me...she sounded like Nicole had in the alley.

I rushed to her, still on my knees, blood pounding in my head. I grabbed Suzannah's slender white hand resting on the bedspread and looked her in the eyes.

That wounded-animal look was there, but even more—a glimmer of light, a desire to trust that hope is real.

"Tell me why he let them die," she said.

More tears pricked at my own eyes. "I don't know, Suzannah—I don't know. I just know that I trust him."

Her tone turned teary and high-pitched. "And that's enough for you?"

"Yes." My heart soared to realize it was true—I meant it. "Suzannah, he brought me all the way here. He quodeshed me, without Grandpa Mack, around so many states and even did it without an exit where I would smash into a guardrail if he didn't. I needed him and he showed up. I don't know what else to tell you. I trust myself because I trust him."

Silence settled between us. And then I did know what to tell her. "Grow as we go," I whispered.

Suzannah blinked at me, something flickering across the panes of her eyes. "I can't believe this..." Her tone turned soft and twined. "Dennis...he sent me that song a few weeks ago. 'Grow As We Go'? By Ben Platt."

It felt like a ball of string unraveling as she talked. Sunshine broke through the window to my right and warmed the tears drying on my face.

A beam spread across my face, literally from ear to ear. "So are you going to get married today?" I asked when Suzannah paused.

Her mouth dropped open.

"You don't need to be afraid," I added gently—the way Grandpa Mack would. Maybe the way Mom would too, if she were here.

Suzannah shot to her feet. "It's a shame my makeup is a mess! What time is it?"

DENNIS'S MOM HAD THIN SKIN you could see the veins through, which were a pale porcelain blue beneath her wrists.

She shivered underneath a shawl woven with the colors of the ocean.

I had thrown on my bridesmaid dress in thirty seconds, and it now stuck to the dried sweat all over me. I hadn't had time to shower or cover my wounds with makeup, of course.

Ava had and she looked fresh standing beside me at the altar.

The backyard awning Dennis and Suzannah would take their vows under was a white wooden lattice laden with vines and lilacs. It was buried in the ground, without a raised platform for the preacher or wedding party to stand on, because this was more "aesthetically pleasing."

My lilac bridesmaid dress fit me to a T.

I liked the rest of the design, but the slit along my leg had come a little higher than I was comfortable with, so when it had arrived Grandpa Mack had told me I could take it to Miss Eunice and ask her to teach me how to use a needle and thread.

Even though she forgot my parents were dead sometimes, she loved to mother me. The newly sewn slit fell at the right length along my leg.

When I'd met Adam—the groomsman who had walked down the aisle with me—he had looked me up and down with a smile too big for his face and offered me his arm.

I had actually appreciated his support as we walked the aisle because I was wobbly in heels. We had parted after walking past all the white chairs with flowers tied to them.

Walking towards the beach and the bright blue horizon had felt like quodeshing, like walking towards a twinkling opening in the sky. Dennis had smiled at me as I took my place.

Now everyone waited for the bride.

The guests spread across the huge backyard, as many flowers as people.

Wind from the beach at our backs blew my limp hair into my face.

The ring bearer came down the aisle. It was one of Dennis's cousins riding a red-and-yellow trike. The little boy wore a suit which bunched around his knees as he pedaled the trike one slow stroke at a time. Somebody had obviously told him to pedal slowly, as he glanced to the side every now and then.

When he reached the last couple feet, he put on a burst of speed with a mischievous smile and everyone laughed.

He put on the brakes with his feet, little brown buckled shoes hitting the grass hard, and stopped in front of Adam and James. He stood, fumbled with the knots tying the ring pillow to the back of the trike, and eventually handed them over to James, who stood closest to Dennis.

The rings shimmered in the sunlight as James held them. The

black vines and kite-shaped diamond of Suzannah's ring glittered next to a simple black gold band for Dennis.

I didn't know who the pastor was, but he flipped through his notes serenely. Not quite at the stage of gray hair yet, he'd still probably seen *many* weddings.

A tiny little girl holding Daphne's hand and hiding her face in the lilac skirt of Daphne's dress started up the aisle next.

Daphne, the maid of honor, wore the same lilac dress as us bridesmaids—a square neckline, slit up the right thigh, silky fabric...very "aesthetically pleasing."

Daphne tapped the little girl's hand.

The girl held a basket of black wood filled with purple rose petals. Her little lips twisted in fear, but she tossed the petals in the air after Daphne grabbed a few handfuls and threw them for her.

The wedding march came on with a *da-dun-da-dun*. Everyone stood, dresses rustling in announcement of Suzannah's presence.

She'd redone the makeup, and the sunshine lit up her red braid and the flowers woven through it, but even more beautiful than that was her smile like rippling water after a storm. Her arm intertwined with Grandpa Mack's.

Grandpa Mack wore his suit, looking like a sailor. A white handkerchief emerged from his breast pocket where he had held the ring before.

He kissed Suzannah on the cheek before he handed her off and his eyes glittered like diamonds with unshed tears. He sat next to Dennis's parents with a quiet word of greeting.

Suzannah and Dennis clasped hands at the altar, their eyes speaking tales from the hours and hours of separation this morning.

"You look stunning, gorgeous, rapturous..." Dennis whispered.

Suzannah beamed and tugged his lilac tie straight with her free hand.

They faced the pastor together.

With every vow, every "I do," every sniffle in the crowd, my heart swelled to bursting. When they exchanged rings, Ava and I made eye contact. I grinned so hard the scratch on my cheek burned.

Grandpa Mack pulled his handkerchief from his pocket and sopped up some tears with it.

The pastor announced, "You may now kiss the bride."

Dennis and Suzannah took a good long time with their kissing and the photographer's shutter *snap-snap-snapped.*

They broke off and the pastor raised his hands. "I present to you Mr. and Mrs. Thatcher!" Suzannah pulled Dennis down the aisle, and he went laughing as the pastor continued: "Please go inside for light refreshments while the wedding party takes pictures."

And suddenly Adam and James beckoned Ava and I over to the gate separating the backyard from the beach.

"Smile!" the photographer called.

I looked up, the seaward wind catching my reddish curls and sending them reeling in the air, catching the skirt of my dress and ruffling it.

When it was my turn to take one-on-one photos with the bride, Suzannah made eye contact and reached for me. We stood several feet away from each other, but I held out my hand and the photographer went *snap, snap, snap* as we reached without connecting.

Then Suzannah closed the distance and clasped her hand in mine, our eyes locked on each other the whole time.

The last picture we took was of our family—me, Suzannah, and Grandpa Mack...holding a framed picture of our parents.

After he handed the photo back to the maid of honor, Grandpa Mack dabbed his eyes and wrapped Suzannah up in a hug.

I dropped my bouquet and joined them.

My heart still felt all full of emotions as us bridesmaids and groomsmen formed an archway with our hands between the backyard and the grand reception room.

Dennis led Suzannah through the archway while everyone cheered.

The room had huge windows and white walls, and in the center of it stood a three-layer white cake with a bride and groom cake topper dancing amid a field of violets.

He fed her the cake first, smudging white frosting on her lips.

Then she fed him a bite. As he licked his lips, she pointed to the smudge on her mouth, waiting for him to wipe it off.

He used his finger instead of a napkin and she screeched. "For love and shame, Dennis!"

She threw the bouquet after that, and as hard as Ava tried, someone else caught it. I have no idea who, partly because I wasn't watching, and partly because the person who walked away with it I'd never seen before in my life.

For dinner, everyone moved to the lawn, which had been reset with white tables.

A tiny, wrapped package lay on top of each place setting. A breath mint was inside each one. They read: "Dennis and Suzannah, Mint to Be" in big letters and "Thanks for Celebrating with Us" in small script.

The caterers served a creamy lemon chicken with penne pasta and some sort of broccoli dish. It was really nice to sit down and enjoy fancy food after the last twenty-four hours of slapdash meals on the road. I ate every last scrap.

After dinner, the party moved inside again.

Hazel and I munched on cake while we watched Suzannah and Dennis dance. "Do you think parties will be like this in college?" I asked her as "Y.M.C.A." came on. A couple rounds of wine had been served already, and some couples were tripping over each other.

"No clue." Hazel licked icing from her fingers. It had turned her fingers the same blue as her polka-dotted dress. "I'm not going."

I laughed and popped a delicate frosting flower in my mouth.

Grandpa Mack approached us just as the music switched to a jazzy song. "Hazel, how's yer car?"

Hazel smiled and lowered her icing-covered fingers. "Good."

Grandpa Mack lowered his head. "Praise the Lord you young folks made it fer the wedding." Then he turned to me and bowed. "May I have this dance?"

I grinned with icing-covered teeth and gave him my hand. He twirled me for ages and ages on the dance floor, finally pulling me close to him for a slow song. We'd been laughing, but as he held me close, I started to cry.

Tears welled from a storeroom in my chest and poured from my eyes.

His beard rustled against my hair as he rested his hand on my shoulder. "What's wrong, Lauren?"

I tilted back my head, my cheek against his chest, and flicked my eyes upward to him and the piece of sky in the corner of my vision. The sun was settling over the horizon to dash shades of red over the ocean. "I'm just so happy that I'm here with you. That we got here safely with the ring."

"Yer a good leader."

I lowered my face. His suit jacket smelled musty. "I failed sometimes."

"But ya made it."

From the corner of my eye, I glimpsed Ava hanging on Xavier's shoulders, swaying more haphazardly than intentionally.

"I'm just so glad it's over."

Grandpa Mack's beard tickled my forehead even more as he leaned down to kiss my brow. "Yer journey ain't over, sweetheart. It's jest begun."

Be a friend to the community of readers.
Help other readers find books they'll love
by leaving an honest review of *Beyond the Mirage*
on Amazon or Goodreads.

Even one sentence helps, nothing fancy required!

ACKNOWLEDGMENTS

DEAR READER, I'm amazed that you're holding this book in your hands. Thank you for giving my story a chance! I'm praying right now that it encourages you to trust God, and in that context, trust yourself.

If you enjoyed this book (or even if you didn't), could you take a few minutes to review it on Amazon and/or Goodreads? It works wonders for reaching other readers who might love it. I really can't get this book in their hands without you.

Before I go any further, I need to thank Jesus. You are what's true, Lord, and I'm so grateful.

I also need to thank a whole host of other people:

Jack. You're one of the kindest gifts God's ever given me. Thanks for making this happen in so many practical ways, and for letting me launch a book in our first year of marriage.

Thank you, Mom, Dad, Adi, and Reed. I never could've gotten here without your support. I love you so much!

Thank you, Brad and Melissa, for teaching me to write from my wholeness.

To my production team/publishing home: It's an incredible honor to be part of *The Pearl* family. You all are amazing, thank you for shaping this book into what it is now. Thank you for shaping me into a better reflection of Jesus too. Special thanks to the kind residents of Casey, Illinois.

This is my debut novel. Just like Lauren, I don't know what's next, but I'm excited. Because when you trust a good God, every unknown part of the future shimmers with possibility. I hope you stay for the next book, dear reader, because our journey isn't over. In fact, it's jest beginning.

Until next time,

Vella Karman

ABOUT THE AUTHOR

VELLA KARMAN is a story addict and novelist drawing on her southern roots to craft stories splashed with color and emotion.

Her writing has been read in more than forty countries so far and she aspires to write gripping, whimsical stories that keep readers up till three a.m.

She's a graduate of The Company apprenticeship and the creative mind behind the *Fantastical Summer* anthology. Her work has also appeared in *The Wanderer's Post* in the UK and *The Pearl* online magazine.

When she isn't crafting stories, you can find her helping people fill their lives with LIGHT on her website and cultivating community on Instagram. Go find out what else she's up to at vellakarman.com!

MORE MAGICAL STORIES FROM

VELLA KARMAN

A mermaid outcast, a girl who can steal stars, and a teenager who grows a tail when she's embarrassed —these are just a few of the fantastical premises you'll find in this collection of clean short stories.

SCAN OR SEARCH "FANTASTICAL SUMMER" WHEREVER BOOKS ARE SOLD!

LOOKING FOR ANOTHER

GREAT YA NOVEL?

"A thrilling ride through time and page...a novel that pulls at the heartstrings and captures the pain of growing up and letting go."

THIRZAH
Author of *Adventures in Eldnaire*

SCAN OR SEARCH "CALL IT CONSEQUENCES" WHEREVER BOOKS ARE SOLD!

WANT TO WRITE LIKE VELLA?

Vella Karman is a graduate of The Company's full-time writing apprenticeship.

The apprenticeship is a college-alternative for motivated Christian writers. Our full-time, in-person program turns passionate young writers into published authors.

If you're ready to kick your writing into gear, learn more at: **Writers.Company**

WE HAVE SO MUCH MORE FOR YOU!

PEARLMAG.CO

Visit us and subscribe at PearlMag.co:

- New short stories, poetry, and essays regularly published online (all free!)
- More books to explore from genre-bending Christian authors
- Opportunities to submit your stories and connect with other readers

www.ingramcontent.com/pod-product-compliance
Lightning Source LLC
LaVergne TN
LVHW091143080826
845145LV00008B/2238

* 9 7 8 1 9 6 0 2 3 0 2 5 6 *